# YOU SLEIGH ME

## CAPRICORN COVE SERIES

### EVIE MITCHELL

THUNDER THIGHS PUBLISHING

Editor: Nicole Wilson, Evermore Editing
http://www.evermoreediting.wixsite.com/info
Illustrations by Laras Putri

# ACKNOWLEDGEMENT OF COUNTRY

I acknowledge the Traditional Custodians of the lands on which I write, the Ngunnawal people, and pay my respect to elders both past and present.

I acknowledge the continued and deep spiritual relationship of the Australian Aboriginal and Torres Strait Islander peoples' to this land, and their unique cultural and spiritual relationships to the land, waters and seas and their rich contribution to society.

**Always was, always will be.**

*For my husband.*
*Thanks for not killing me during a pandemic. I now*
*know the meaning of true love is wearing a mask*
*and drowning in disinfectant.*
*Love you.*

# YOU SLEIGH ME

**Farrah**

I need a million dollars. I don't have even ten bucks in my bank, but I need a cool million by Christmas if I want to save the town's wildlife reserve.

Enter Wolf Rodriguez, local good boy, international heartthrob, and lead singer of Metal Heart the hottest band in the world.

Oh, and my ex-high school crush.

I just have to convince him to help me pull off the fundraiser of a lifetime... even if being around the attractive rocker turns me into a bumbling, blushing fool.

Turns out, Wolf likes that kind of thing.

**Wolf**

This holiday I just wanted to spoil my niece,

eat some pie and recharge. God, did I need to recharge. The last four years had been nothing but tours, records and screaming fans. With the new year fast approaching, I had songs to produce for our new album.

Pity my muse is missing in action.

Or at least it was, until I overheard Farrah Sharif whispering to a stuffed turtle. The cadence of her voice, her tone, her words – all of it is revving my muse into overdrive.

So, we strike a deal, in exchange for performing at her charity gig, Farrah has to let me record her voice.

Only, I didn't expect to crave every mention of my name on her lips.

She's slaying me. And I can't help but love how bad it hurts.

*Warning: This book is inspired by hot rock stars, ASMR, and the joy that only a good Christmas story can bring. So, escape the craziness, find someone to kiss under the mistletoe, and give yourself the gift of a great holiday read.*

# 1

**Farrah**

I pressed sweaty palms to my plaid skirt while mentally rehearsing my pitch.

*Mister Charles, thank you for seeing me. As you would be aware, your father was a long-term supporter of the Capricorn Cove Wildlife Education and Rehabilitation Centre. In his honour, we've—*

"He's ready to see you now," the receptionist interrupted my silent practice.

"Thank you." I picked up my bag, which contained my proposal, sucking in a deep breath and squaring my shoulders.

*You can do this, Farrah. You've done this a hundred times before. You've got this.*

I may have entered a million offices just like

this one, knocking on doors and asking for donations to assist us in continuing to run the Centre, but never had it been more crucial than at this moment.

COVID-19 had drastically reduced our donor base. Over the two years since it had first hit, we'd had more than half our operating budget slashed, which meant that our little Centre was struggling – big time.

Inside the room sat Mr. Charles the younger, the impressive view of the city at his back.

*Guess the company's still going well enough to afford top floor position.*

That had to be a good sign. Mr. Charles' father had been our biggest donor for the last five years, contributing over a million dollars to our operating budget. Sadly, Mr. Charles Senior had passed, leaving his son to take over the company.

I'd met the son a few times and been rather underwhelmed during each interaction.

"Mr. Charles." I held out my hand, striding confidently towards the desk. "Thank you for seeing me."

"Ms. Sharif." He accepted my handshake but didn't invite me to sit.

*Uh-oh.*

"I see no reason to keep you for longer than

necessary." He cleared his throat, looking down at the papers on his desk as he delivered the news. "Rattler Industries won't be supporting your little Centre any longer. We've decided to shift our philanthropic efforts in another direction."

I blinked, attempting to process his words. "I... I'm sorry?"

"We won't be contributing any financial support to your Centre."

I swear I heard the tires screeching and the smashed steel and glass of a car crash, followed by the horrified screams of all my employees as I destroyed our work.

"Mr. Charles, sir. Please, a whole wing of our Centre is named after Rattler Industries. You're our biggest donor. I can appreciate that you—"

"My mind is made up." He straightened, buttoning his suit jacket. "If you'll excuse me, I have another appointment."

In a daze, I left his office, stumbling past the sympathetic gaze of his secretary and out to the elevator. I slapped at the button, staring unblinkingly at the numbers as they counted up to my floor.

*The animals. My staff. The turtle extension. Oh my gods, the turtle extension! What am I going to do?*

The elevator doors slid open, and I stepped

in, turning automatically and staring at the closing doors.

"Ground?" The cart guy asked.

"Um, yeah, thanks."

*They're rich enough to afford a building that has a guy whose sole duty is to press buttons in an elevator.*

The shock wore off, reality hitting me like a punch to the guts.

I'd put this trip on my credit card, spending money I didn't have in hopes this would be our saving grace. I'd devoted hours of my own time developing my proposal. I'd bought a fancy, itchy suit and kept the tags, knowing I'd need to return it once I got home.

*Oh Gods, this is going to ruin us.*

The elevator doors slid open, admitting another passenger.

I shuffled back, staring down at the pointed toes of my borrowed heels. The damned things pinched like the dickens, but I'd done it. I'd squeezed my giant ass feet into these tiny fucking heels in hopes of impressing a man who hadn't even invited me to sit down.

*Fuck you, Mr. Charles Jr. Fuck your fucking face, you fucking fuck faced asshole!*

Thinking it didn't make me feel any better.

The elevator stopped again, letting out passengers and taking on new ones.

*I hate these shoes.*

Anger gave way to despair, tears stinging the backs of my eyes.

*I've let my staff down.*

We'd signed up for the build three years ago. Mr. Charles and other donors had generously contributed to phase one and indicated that they'd continue to do so. By phase two, I'd expected to have all the donors lined up.

No one had expected COVID to hit. The pandemic had dried up my donations, and people were no longer willing to part with their hard-won cash.

The elevator dinged again, the doors sliding open once more.

"Farrah?"

I looked up, blinking through the shimmer of tears.

"Wolf?"

He grinned, entering the lift, holding his elbow out for a bump.

I'd last seen him, he'd been dressed as incognito Spiderman for Halloween – and I'd made out with him briefly. I blamed the cheap wine and nostalgia.

Since then, I'd seen him floating around Capricorn Cove, our hometown, and somehow managed to avoid crossing paths. I still felt embarrassed about that kiss though I knew I had no reason to be.

Today he looked every inch the hot rock star, with his perfect amount of scruff, his slightly too-long hair, and the glint of devilish mischief in his eye.

I lifted my elbow, bumping it with his, trying to put on a brave face as I noticed his leather jacket.

*Probably cost more than I earnt last year.*

"What are you doing here?" he asked as his entourage filled the lift.

"I could say the same about you." I tried for a smile, knowing it fell flat.

He searched my face, his gaze growing concerned. "Are you okay?"

My breath caught, the weight of my failure punching me in the gut. "I'm... no."

"Wolf?" The PA beside him held up a phone. "It's Glenn, he needs to talk to you about the—"

Wolf accepted the phone, his gaze still locked on me. "Glenn? Yeah, can I call you back? Great."

He hung up, his face concerned as he continued to stare at me. "You wanna get a coffee? Go somewhere and talk about it?"

I huffed out a wet laugh. "Can rock stars still do that? Just go somewhere and get coffee?"

His lips twitched, a small grin pulling at his

mouth. If a paparazzi had captured that look, I had no doubt they'd be able to sell it to a magazine that millions of young girls read, each cutting out the picture and sticking it to their wall.

*Maybe I should do that? Sell his picture? Surely that would be worth a few bucks.*

I immediately and vehemently rejected the thought. Never would I ever sink to that level.

"We have our ways," he said with a grin.

We reached the ground floor, and the other passengers in the lift, including his people, exited first. For a moment, that left just Wolf, me and the button guy standing in the small space.

"I'm not gonna be good company," I warned, brushing at my cheek, frustrated when I found a stray tear.

"I don't know about that." He reached out, hooking his arm with mine, guiding us into the lobby. "You're definitely better than my last executive-directed date."

I lifted an eyebrow in question.

Wolf laughed, giving an exaggerated shudder as he guided me across the lobby. "Long story short, it was a favour to a friend of my agent. The girl climbed across the table halfway through dinner and attempted to cut a piece of my hair with a butter knife."

I laughed, shaking my head. "Dude, your life is so weird."

"Don't I know it."

Outside cameras flashed, capturing what would, for anyone else, have been an intimate moment between old-school friends.

"Ignore them," he muttered, taking my hand and ploughing us through the gathering. "My car's over here."

Sure enough, a town car idled by the curb, Wolf's bodyguard clearing a path. He pulled the door open, holding it for us as Wolf dropped my hand, his palm putting pressure on my lower back, guiding me passed him and helping me into the car. He followed a moment later, the guard rounding the car and getting in the front.

"What about your entourage?" I asked as bulbs flashed against the tinted windows, no doubt capturing Wolf and me mid-buckle.

*How interesting that picture must be. Not.*

He flicked a thumb over his shoulder. "Second car."

Our transport pulled away from the curb, merging with the traffic.

"Where to?" the driver asked.

"Benson's. Thanks, Jim."

"Benson's?"

Wolf shot me a smile. "It's an exclusive club. Invite only. Think of it like a place where the rich and famous can go to chill out. No phones, no cameras, and no bodyguards required. Safe, secure and private."

I shook my head. "I honestly don't know how you live like this. It seems more like a prison than a pleasure."

Wolf blew out a breath, his lips quirking at one corner. "Some days it is. Then I stand in front of a packed stadium listening as they sing my words back to me, words I've crafted, drafted and sung, and I remember why I do this."

I reached out, giving his arm a squeeze. "I always knew you were a singer."

He chuckled, leaning back in his seat, his easy smile as familiar to me as my own. "Yeah?"

"Mm." I nodded, glancing away, finding myself too distracted by the warmth in his familiar eyes. "I mean, your rendition of Gomez in the Addams Family musical was pretty awesome."

He laughed, the sound rich and rolling. "Well, if high school musicals are anything to go by, then you should be the queen of darkness with your stunning performance of Morticia."

His eyes flashed, and I wondered if he remembered Halloween night when we'd stolen kisses.

*Warm beer, hot kisses, the cool of the night. His hand on my breast, my fingers pulling the Spiderman mask from his head. A noise. A scramble. A moment interrupted.*

During high school, we'd been friends without a lick of chemistry between us. Or at least none on his part. Me? I'd been a bundle of hormonal longing for young Wolf. But necessity and the knowledge that Wolf lived way outside my league had kept me in check.

But his return to Capricorn Cove had ushered in a new dynamic in our acquaintance – a sexual simmering that shimmered between us like the haze of heat on a hot summer's day.

"We're here."

I glanced at the bodyguard who'd spoken, the car rolling to a stop in front of a nondescript building. It blended with the others in this neighbourhood, an apartment building that had seen better days.

"Is this it?" I asked, unclicking my seat belt.

"Yep. Trust me, its façade is a ruse for what's inside."

We exited the car, Wolf rounding it to place a hand on my lower back, guiding me inside. The lobby was as innocuous as the exterior, cheap white tile, a few patchy leather seats, a bay of elevators and an old wooden reception desk. The only inkling that all was not as it seemed were the three men seated behind the desk. Where most buildings might have one elderly doorman, this place had three strapping young men all watching us with practised looks of suspicion.

Wolf pulled his wallet from his back pocket, flicking it open to remove a small card. He pressed it to a sensor resting on the desk, the sensor making a small ding of approval.

"Mr. Rodriguez, welcome back." One of the guards greeted, looking from his computer to us. "Are you bringing a guest with you today?"

"Yep."

The guard nodded, and a second one reached for a tablet, unlocking it and wiping an antibacterial cloth across the screen before handing it to me.

"The contract and non-disclosure are there. We require your ID, a signature, and a thumbprint."

I lifted my handbag, digging through the mess to pull my purse free and find my ID.

He scanned it in as I read through the terms and conditions.

"Holy hell," I breathed, my eyes bugging out at the penalties listed. "Wolf, this is insane."

"Privacy costs." He shrugged. "We can go somewhere else if this makes you uncom-fortable."

"No, no, it's fine."

I pressed my thumb to the tablet, the screen scanning it in.

"Here you go, Ms. Sharif." The second guard handed me back my ID. "A copy of the contract will be emailed to you shortly, but you're good to head up."

The third guard stood, holding out a clear lock box with a number printed in plain black on the front.

"Phones, cameras, USBs, listening devices, smart watches, anything electronic," the guard rattled off in a bored tone.

I glanced at Wolf but did as directed, dropping my phone into the box.

Done, Wolf led me to the elevator bay, the doors of one cab gliding open. We stepped inside, and my final glimpse of the lobby was one of Wolf's bodyguards leaning against the desk and chatting to the three doormen.

"This is super weird," I finally said, my eyes trained on the ascending numbers flashing on the screen.

"Oh, believe me, I know."

On level three, the doors slid open, revealing a scene so lush, so decadent that for a moment, I wondered if we had been transported to another world.

"Come on, let's get that coffee."

**2**

**Wolf**

I guided Farrah through the lush room, finding myself delighted and amused at her wide-eyed wonder.

> Wasn't so long ago that you'd have had the same look on your face.

> Thanks, Dad.

Some people had an inner voice for their conscience, I had my dad. I knew it wasn't really my father, but after he'd passed, I'd started hearing his voice and begun having silent conversations with him. I'd figured it was my way of keeping a part of him alive.

I like this one, don't scare her off.

This room had to be one of my favourites in Benson's. It had some fancy-pants name, but I called it the Jungle room. Vivid ferns and creeper vines, colourful succulents, and magnificent orchids grew across every surface and up each wall. Brass fixtures and fittings mixed with cane and lush white linen, while the sound of water trickled calmingly in the background.

"This is a café?" Farrah asked, her voice hushed as a parrot flew over our heads to perch on a small platform. It reached with one foot to pluck a sunflower and bring it to its beak to nibble, eyeing us as we passed by.

I found myself pausing, a tickle of pleasurable awareness tingling my scalp in response to the tone of Farrah's words.

*Oh... shit. Not now.*

I cleared my throat, trying not to give into the sensation.

"Benson's is whatever you want it to be."

Her eyebrows lifted. "Sorry, what?"

The tingle intensified as I swept an arm out, encompassing the room. "It's a retreat for the rich and famous. Here we can relax and let our hair down without worrying that someone is going to snap a picture and release it to the media. It can be a café or bar, a workspace or party area. Benson's is whatever we need it to be."

Farrah shook her head, sending her unruly curls bouncing. "You realise this is insane, right?"

"Oh, I know. Money is power, Sharif. If you haven't worked that out by now, then I'm worried for you." I expected a quick reply, a snappy quip about rich people's problems. Instead, Farrah halted, her face stricken.

"Shit, Farrah?"

"I...." Her lip wobbled, eyes filling with tears. "Sorry, I just... sorry. It's been a shitty day."

"Come on." I grabbed her hand, leading her through the jungle to the private area at the back of the room. Tucked behind a cane weave room divider and a curtain made from vines, lay a low table, complete with comfortable seating.

A waiter came and discreetly took our order as Farrah battled against tears. He returned quickly with coffee, cake and a small box of tissues.

"Just press the button here—" The waiter leaned over, gesturing at a discreet touchpad on the side of the table. "—should you need anything else."

With that, he disappeared, fading through the curtain and leaving us alone.

Farrah reached for the tissues, her lashes wet. "Guess I wasn't fooling anyone, huh?"

I cupped my mug, watching her dab at her eyes. "Tell me about it?"

She blew out a breath, defeat carved into every line of her body – even her riot of curls seemed less perky.

"It's been a shitty few years.

I nodded. "I heard about the election. That sucked."

Farrah had been mayor of our small town for a few years before one of the local millionaires had decided to run against her. He'd won not because he was the better candidate but because he had more money to throw at the campaign.

She sighed. "Being Mayor was great, but it's not what I'm upset about. I fucked up a meeting today, and we lost a donor. We might have to close the rescue. No," she corrected, her voice breaking. "We will have to."

I sucked in a breath, my mind whirling.

"The rescue is your life."

She huffed out a sad laugh. "Yeah. Or at least it was. I fucked up, Wolf. I fucked up really, really badly."

I leaned across the table, capturing her hand, entwining our fingers to give her a squeeze. "I doubt it. You're the smartest woman I know."

She shook her head, a tear sliding down her cheek as her breath caught, the sob broken. "Thi-This is one time that th-there's no coming b-b-back. I overcommitted us."

"How?"

She blew out a breath, closing her eyes. "We needed a bigger premise. I got g-g-greedy. I wanted to expand. We were busting at the seams. And the new marina is b-b-bringing tourists, which will give us an opportunity to look at expanding our marine rescue side. I thought we'd be sweet."

"But?"

She let out a long sigh, her voice shaky but no longer stuttering with emotion.

"But COVID-19 hit, and our donors began to dry up. I'd signed a three-phase agreement but only had money for the first two phases. Phase two went over budget thanks to COVID, and the next thing I know, I've got contractors at my door demanding the next payment."

I frowned. "Can't you pull out?"

She shook her head. "We're a not-for-profit, getting anyone to even take us on originally was a feat. I had to sign the contract and pay deposits upfront. We pull out, I still have to pay twenty-five percent."

"How much is left on the contract?"

She swallowed, her face paling. "Just over a million."

"A—" I bit off my surprise, stamping down any judgement. "What happened?"

"The short story is I had a donor lined up. He agreed to take over the whole contract in exchange for naming the turtle rescue after his company." She shook her head. "The week before the payment was due to be transferred to us, he died. I had a meeting with his son today – he's pulled out. They're not honouring the contract."

"That's fucked."

A wet laugh burst free, her lips lifting as if she couldn't help herself. "Yeah, well... I guess that's life, right?"

She detached our fingers, lifting the small teapot to pour chia into the delicate tea cup.

My brain, which had been racing to help her find a solution, stuttered to a halt, focusing in on the sounds she made as she replaced the pot on the table then lifted the cup, taking a sip of the brew.

The sound of her stirring her spoon as it tapped against the sides of the cup, her gentle sip, the soft clack of her cup as Farrah replaced it in the saucer – all of it worked to bring on pleasurable, tingling sensations.

I closed my eyes, giving over to the tingles, my body relaxing, letting go.

*Though the mist of tomorrow, I see you*

*You and your pretty eyes*

*You live in me and....*

Someone cleared their throat across the room, breaking Farrah's hold on me.

*You live in me and...*

*And...*

*God damn it!*

The last time I'd written anything more than a sentence had been the night after Halloween. Listening to Farrah all night, singing with her around the fire, it'd sparked my muse like nothing else had in over a year.

I sighed, pinching the bridge of my nose while I forcefully tossed aside my frustration and focused on Farrah.

"What options do you have?"

She shrugged. "I just don't know."

I opened my mouth to offer advice when we were interrupted.

"Wolf?"

We both looked over, finding a man twice our age pushing through the ferns.

"Glenn? What are you doing here?"

My agent sat down, sparing Farrah a half-glance before turning his full attention to me. "You owe me a song."

Farrah pushed up from her seat, reaching for her coat.

"I should go."

"Farrah, wait—"

"No, you're busy. Sorry. I-I mean—I'll—I've got to get to the airport anyway. I'll see you around."

I caught her hand, halting her escape. "At least use my car. The driver will take you anywhere you need to go."

Her lips pressed together, her head jerking up. "I don't need charity."

I reached forward, brushing a thumb over her still-damp cheek. "It's not charity. Call it a favour. And an apology." I dropped my hand, pulling a card from my back pocket. "Here's his number. I'll be here for another few hours. You'll be doing him a favour by keeping him from sitting in a car playing Candy Crush or some shit."

Her lips quirked. "I doubt that but thank you." She took the card, folding it into her palm.

"I'm in town soon, can we... catch up? Maybe get together to brainstorm some solutions?" I asked, finding myself loathed to let her go.

*That's because she's a friend. An old, dear friend.*

*Mm, and it definitely has nothing to do with the*

*fact you find her both trustworthy, attractive and muse-inspiring.*

Farrah lifted her face, glancing up at me through a curtain of curls, her dark eyes searching and a little surprised.

"You'd be willing to do that?"

"Of course."

Her cheeks flushed, a smile curving her lips. "Okay. You know where to find me."

It was on the tip of my tongue to ask for her number, but she stepped back, breaking the moment.

"Thanks for...." She shrugged. "I guess for just being a good friend. I definitely needed one today."

"Any time."

"Later, Wolf."

"Later."

With that, she pivoted on her heel and disappeared through the vines, leaving behind only the scent of her spicy perfume and an unsettled feeling in my gut.

"Nice girl," Glenn commented, pressing the touchpad to call a waiter. "Now, let's talk business."

I gritted my teeth, knowing there was no escape and pissed as hell that he'd interrupted a moment with Farrah.

> Seems to be a theme with you two.

> Shut it, Dad.

I turned to Glenn, biting down on my frustration. "I already told you, I'm working on it."

"Working on it isn't getting me an album." He leaned forward, his gaze turning paternal. "Talk to me, kid. What's happening? You burnt out?"

I shoved hands through my hair, linking them behind my head, tired of this conversation. "Glenn... Leave it with me. I'll get you the songs."

"By New Year?"

I shrugged. "Sure, let's say that."

Glenn began to drum his fingers against the table. "You better not be bullshitting. I need those songs, Wolf. Or else we're bringing in the ghostwriters."

Unease and frustration slipped down my back, my body clenching. "I'm good. I just need a nap and some inspo."

"And you'll get that here?" Glenn asked, looking pointedly around the room.

I thought of Farrah's stricken face. "Nah, I need to go home."

A waiter appeared, taking Glenn's order before quietly slipping away. The only sounds were from the water feature near the bar and the soft call of animals around us.

And Glenn's nervous beating of his fingers against the tabletop, the sound an unwelcome intrusion. He considered me with an indecipherable expression, continuing to drum until I reached out, stilling his fingers.

The waiter chose that moment to float in, placing a lemonade and a sandwich on the table, then gliding out, leaving us alone once more.

"What?" I finally asked, breaking the silence.

"You tell me, kid. You're the one with your panties in a wad."

This was why I both loved and hated Glenn. He reminded me too much of my dad.

My trip to fame wasn't conventional. I hadn't won any singing show, or put in years of work running around the gig scene. My rise to rock stardom had simply been a result of a series of serendipitous accidents.

I'd been home for the weekend visiting my Ma. I hadn't planned on coming home, but my roommate at College had indicated that he wanted to have a girl over. While I didn't mind sharing a room with him, trying to sleep beside a newly intimate couple wasn't my idea of a good weekend.

During that weekend, one of the local girls, Ella Bronze, had gotten married. The band she'd booked had been stuck out of state, leaving her without any musicians. A friend of a friend of my brother's had called, asking if I was willing to pitch in. They'd remembered that I performed back in my high school days, doing weddings and whatnot to earn some extra cash.

I'd had my guitar on me, so had agreed. I'd figuring that while I might have been a bit rusty performing to a crowd, I surely had to be better than a last-minute playlist someone's aunt threw together.

The wedding had gone without a hitch (apart from the bear, but that was a whole other story), and I'd had a great night.

I'd woken the next morning to a million followers on my social media account.

Turned out, Laura Sweep—the Queen of Clean and reality TV darling—was the groom's sister-in-law. She'd filmed me singing a few songs and posted them to her socials, claiming I'd saved the day.

People had posted requests, and Mum had gotten a kick outta it, so we'd spent the day filming me doing a few plus one original.

I'd thought sure it'd all blow over within twenty-four hours. It hadn't. Within forty-eight hours, I had three offers from record producers and six agents DM'ing me for meetings.

I'd gone back to College only to find that my life had completely changed. People I'd never known before came up to me to chat. People I'd known forever now wanted to talk music and ask me about my next steps.

I'd been invited on three talk shows to sing.

I had a Kardashian ask if I'd be interested in singing at her next gala.

My life had changed. Drastically.

Enter Glenn.

I'd met four agents before Glenn had reached out. My brother, Tristan, happened to be the owner of the best bullshit detector this side of the equator. Pretty handy, considering he was Capricorn Cove's Sheriff. He'd rejected everyone that'd come before Glenn.

Glenn had walked in, introduced himself then immediately laid it all out.

"I don't deal with divas or douchebags. You're my client, I expect results. You get three passes. Third strike, you're out." He handed me a bound booklet. "I don't work Friday nights through Monday unless there's a gig or some-thing important on. If I do, then I take time off during the week. My family comes first. I don't hear from you those days unless you're in jail, being arrested, in hospital or have killed someone. Other than that, you can call the ten assistants I have on call at all hours. They'll sort you out and decide if I need to be contacted. My contract is in there. I'd recommend getting a lawyer to check it over first." He'd hesitated. "And if you go with someone else, make sure they don't sign anything from Wagner Jones. The real terms of the recording contract are buried in the fine print. It's a shit fight. You won't own anything for decades, and the royalties aren't worth the time you'd take to sign your name on that contract."

With that, he'd left. We'd done as directed, getting a lawyer to check over the contract then signed with Glenn.

We'd interviewed musicians the following week, building a band. Just over a month later, we were in a recording studio, and it had been an upward ride ever since.

"Wolf, talk to me."

Glenn's gentle prod shook me free of my funk.

"I just need a rest," I said, cupping my still-warm coffee mug. "It's been a fucking rough year."

"And you miss your family."

"Yeah."

My heart ached a little just thinking of everything I'd missed while out on the road.

Nicole, my little niece, grew more precocious and free-spirited every day. I wanted to be there to see her grow, to help guide her and love on her.

*She needs a pony.*

*She doesn't need a goddamned pony.*

My dad's voice snapped back, but I ignored it, rapidly calculating whether I could afford a horse plus upkeep.

*Actually...*

"Glenn?"

"Mm?"

"You're better with finances, can I afford to donate a million or two to a charity?"

Glenn coughed, rubbing at his mouth. "Can you... kid, do you know what you're worth?"

I shrugged. "Not really."

Glenn shook his head. "Wolf, I know you're not one for worldly possessions, but seriously. You gotta get your finances in order. Sit down with your accountant and the advisor I set you up with."

"So that's a yes?"

"Son, that's a fuck yes. Last year you personally earned only fifty million less than Ed-fuck-ing-Sheeran. You're big news."

*Huh.*

*Told you to pay more attention to your net worth.*

I shushed my dad, knowing I needed to get my head in the game, but I hated that side of it. I just wanted to write and play.

*Only now you're stuck with no words and a head full of jumbled notes.*

I shoved up from the table. "Can you organise to transfer two, actually make it five million, to the Capricorn Cove Wildlife Education and Rehabilitation Centre? I'll sign whatever needs to happen."

"Sure. It'll take a few weeks through."

"It needs to happen before Christmas."

Glenn narrowed his eyes at me. "This got anything to do with that girl?"

I shrugged. "Does it matter?"

"Don't lose your muse."

"I won't," I lied, walking away from the table.

*Too late, the muse is already gone.*

**3**

**Wolf**

My mobile rang, interrupting my attempted meditation.

With a sigh, I unfolded from my spot on the deck of my house, reaching for the annoying electronic.

CALLER ID: HONEY

My heart jumped, my finger thumbing the screen as I jerked the phone to my ear. "What's happened?"

Honey's familiar laugh tipped down the phone. "Nothing! I just wanted to see if you were still keen to take Nic to kids' hour at the Wildlife Centre before she sleeps over? I'm happy to just drop her by after if you're busy."

My heart calmed, the knot in my stomach receding.

*So much for meditation relaxing you.*

"Nope, not busy. I'll come over in about an hour if that works?"

"Sounds great!"

We hung up, and I stretched, looking out at my view.

Years ago, I'd never have even dared contemplate owning a property like this one. I'd resigned myself to a decent house in suburbia that was close enough to the ocean I could walk but far enough I could afford it.

This? This property went beyond my wildest dreams.

From the solar panel and water-friendly roof to the basement that collected geothermal heat, every inch had been designed with my input. It'd been my first major purchase once I'd paid off my mom's house. I'd bought the vacant block for a steal, building the eco-friendly home.

I could have lived anywhere in the world, but I'd returned to Capricorn Cove, the only place my heart would ever be. This is where my family lived, where my memories of my dad lingered. There couldn't be any other place for me.

With a last glance at the ocean, I walked

through my house, pressing the intercom button.

"Yo?"

"Are one of you free?" I asked, hating that I now required bodyguards to walk around my own town.

"We're all good. How many you need?"

"Just one. I'm taking Nic to kids' hour at the Education Centre."

There was a brief pause before Alec replied. "You've got me and Omar. Hate to say it, boss man, kids' hour might seem innocent, but you've been mobbed by soccer mums before."

I shuddered remembering the bookstore in London. "Fair call. See you in thirty."

My house contained five bedrooms, three bathrooms, two large living areas, a kickass kitchen, a library, a media room, and a massive deck. Spread across three levels, I'd designed it with family in mind.

Additionally, I had a garage which included a secondary residence where my bodyguards lived, a pool, and a gym. I also had a small recording studio that I'd built last year when I'd found myself frustrated by the commute between here and the city.

Clean and looking mildly presentable, I met Alec and Omar at the garage.

"Keys." Omar held out his hand.

"Dude, fuck off. I get to drive less than three percent of the year. Don't take this from me."

He laughed, dropping his hand. "Don't get a ticket, Glenn'll kill me."

We piled into the car, Alec sliding in beside Nic's car seat in the back.

I had a room in my house just for Nicole. I loved my little niece more than I'd ever thought possible, and was determined to be an active participant in her life. When I was in town, we had sleepovers, watched Disney movies and reenacted various songs.

The guys gave me shit, ribbing me about wanting to be a dad, but I couldn't deny it. If there was a male equivalent for exploding ovaries, I had it.

I drove the few miles to my brother's house, finding Honey standing with Nic on their porch. A porch which looked like the entrance to Santa's workshop. Reindeer and elves decorated the lawn while toys and presents in various stages of assembly were scattered around the yard.

No one would ever accuse Honey of not having the Christmas spirit.

"Hey, kiddo!" I called, jumping out of the car.

"Wo-wo!" Nic screamed, jumping up and down, Honey barely holding her back.

"She's a bit excited," Honey laughed as I swept Nic up in my arms, swinging her around.

"Tubles!" she babbled, her little arms flapping out at her side. She wore a Christmas sweater complete with flashing reindeer nose and candy-cane tights that I had no doubt matched a pair her mother owned.

My sister-in-law defined festive.

"That's right." I tucked her into my side, my heart melting as her little arms wrapped around my neck. "Hey, Sis."

I leaned in, giving Honey a kiss on the cheek.

"You better be prepared for this. No take backs, Mister." She waggled her finger at me, a grin on her face as she handed over Nic's overnight bag. "Your brother and I have a date night all planned out."

"Oh, I'm sure you do." I gave her a cheeky wink, to which she blushed, her hand shooting out to slap at my arm.

"Wolf!"

"Wo-wo!" Nic agreed, bouncing in my arms.

"Alright, General Nicole, say farewell to Mommy. We're off to see the turtles."

"Tubles!"

Honey made a big show of kissing her baby girl. "Bye, my darling, be good for Uncle Wolf!"

Nicole, chattering a mile a minute, waved her mother off as I buckled her into the car seat.

"Ready?"

"Set, go!" she yelled, throwing her arms up and kicking her feet.

Omar chuckled, shaking his head. "This kid kills me."

We made it to the Centre with only one demand for ice cream.

"Later," I promised her. "Kids hour first. You wanna see the turtles, right?"

At the Centre, kids ran around screaming bloody murder while volunteers attempted to corral them with limited success.

"Aren't you—?"

"Nope," I said cheerfully, cutting the woman off. "But I get that all the time."

Nicole joined the fracas, her earsplitting screams of joy joining the cacophony of sound emanating from the tiny humans racing around.

"This is worse than that time in Amsterdam," Omar muttered, watching the crazed kids.

"I don't know, that time they didn't have soggy diapers," Alec pointed out. "And the riot only lasted for like thirty minutes, tops."

"Ah-ten-tion!" snapped a voice from across the room.

Everyone in the room, kids, volunteers, parents, even my guards, straightened, the noise fading into silence.

Farrah, dressed as a pirate, complete with a jacket I recognised from her Halloween costume, stalked into the room. On her shoulder sat a seagull with one leg and peeking out of her breast pocket was a small hedgehog. With a sweep of her arm, she encompassed the messy kids' room.

"Are you my swashbuckling crew?"

"Yes!" screamed the kids.

"Well! Let's start with a song, shall we?"

The kids began to bounce up and down, their little bodies barely containing their excitement. Music began to pipe over the speakers as Farrah's husky voice began to sing.

"When I was one, I'd just begun the day I went to sea. I jumped aboard a pirate ship, and the Captain said to me: 'We're going this way, that way, forwards backwards, over the deep blue sea. A bottle of rum to fill my tum, and that's the life for me'."

She followed each action with a movement which the kids echoed, and I saw exactly what she was attempting to do, wear out the initial excitement enough to settle them down.

*Well played, Sharif.*

After the tenth verse, the music ended, the parents clapped, and Farrah gestured for the kids to take a seat. They did so, their little bodies heaving in gasps of air, smiles bright on sweaty faces.

"Alright, me hearties. Now, can anyone tell me what this is on my shoulder?"

Around the room, little hands shot into the air, some of the small kids yelling out answers.

"Yes, you?" Farrah said, pointing at a small boy.

"It's a seagull."

"That's right! Her name is Peg, and she only has one leg and an injured wing."

Farrah explained to the children that Peg had been injured by an animal and, due to her no longer being able to fly, had become a permanent resident of the Centre.

"Would anyone like to give Peg a little pat?" she asked, laughing when all hands shot up.

"Alright, how about you, you and you?"

The three chosen kids jumped up, racing to the front of the room. Under Farrah's guidance, they gently patted the bird, all of them remaining calm while doing so before leaping away to rush to the parents with squeals of delight.

The show went on, with Farrah expertly controlling the little ones while volunteers brought in different animals for the kids to see. Including an old tortoise, sending Nicole into fits of wordless excitement, her arms flapping out at her side.

"I think that's it for today," Farrah said with an exaggerated yawn. "I don't think there's anyone else for us to visit with."

"Tuble!" Nicole wailed, throwing her arms in the air. "Tuble, tuble, tuble!"

"Oh!" Farrah nodded, placing a finger to her chin. "You're right. We haven't seen a turtle to-day. Can anyone see him?"

The monitor behind Farrah lit with an image of a turtle, the children screeching as they pointed at it. She whirled, the screen going dark.

"There's no turtle there!" she cried, shaking her head at the kids.

The screen relit with the image.

"Turtle!" the kids screamed, pointing behind her again.

This went on for several minutes, Farrah stalking around the room to look under shelves and lifting kids up to check under their pillows, sending them into fits of laughter.

Finally, she ducked her head out the door, coming back in with a giant stuffed turtle. "Here he is!"

"Tuble!" Nicole screamed, her eyes practically rolling back in her head with joy.

The kids crowded around, gently stroking

the fake turtle as Farrah explained about how they swam, what their shell was used for and what they liked to eat.

"Now, this one is very fluffy, but the one you saw on the screen is much tougher. More like Hector, the tortoise we met earlier." She leaned down, pretending to listen to the stuffed turtle. "What's that? You have to go?"

Omar elbowed me, catching my attention. He lifted his chin, tipping it to the far side of the room. "Third from the right."

I watched Nicole, subtly turning my head that way when one of the kids darted in that direction. A woman in the crowd of parents had her phone out filming me. She wasn't even looking at the kids.

I looked away, turning myself slightly, blocking her from getting anything but my back. This happened all the time, there was nothing I could do about it, but it still pissed me the fuck off. Here I was with my niece having a great time, and someone had to go ruin it because I'd sung a few songs they liked.

The price of fame, son. You know this. Don't be ungrateful.

I know. It's just hard sometimes.

"Oi! You!" Farrah's voice cut through the noise, bringing all attention to her.

Farrah lifted from the kids, pointing at the woman. "Can't you read?" She turned, pointing angrily at the no photography sign stuck to the wall.

The woman flushed, dropping her hand but still clutching the phone. "I'm not filming the kids, just—"

"Nope," Farrah cut her off with a quick shake of her head. "Hand it over." She held her hand out, and the woman automatically gave her the phone.

Farrah made quick work of it, shaking her head. "Honestly, we have this rule for a reason. These aren't your kids; you don't have permission to be taking pictures of them. I don't need that kind of lawsuit landing on either of our heads." She finished with the phone, handing it back.

The woman grabbed her kid, beating a hasty retreat as one of the other volunteers wrapped up the event, singing a final song with the worn-out kids.

"Look dude, I don't wanna tell you what to do, but... if you don't at least ask her out for coffee, then I will," Alec muttered from my side, his gaze on Farrah.

*Oh, I'm asking her for more than that.*

**4**

**Wolf**

I handed a sleepy Nicole over to Alec.

"Can you hold her for a second?"

He took my precious cargo, wrapping her in his arms. "You gonna find Farrah?"

I nodded, glancing towards the door that read *Staff Only*.

"Good. I'll get the car ready but take Omar with you, he can run interference on any interruptions."

I caught one of the staff as she packed up the mess left by the kids, cleaning each of the toys with disinfectant spray.

"Could you tell me where Farrah is?"

"Oh sure, you can go through that door then down the hall. About halfway down, there's a blue door marked storage. It's our dressing room slash office slash all-purpose room. She'll be in there."

"Thanks."

"No problem... Wolf."

Five years ago, her use of my name might have had me asking if we knew each other. Three years ago, it might have had me questioning what she wanted. Now, it didn't even register, such was my life.

I pushed through the door, finding the hall empty.

"You go, I'll make sure no one bothers you," Omar promised, setting up beside the entrance. "Holla if you need anything."

I nodded, finding the door and pushing it open slowly. Shelving dominated the space, boxes and clear storage containers neatly lined up, each labelled for easy reference.

"Farrah?"

She didn't answer. I pushed through, letting the door click shut behind me.

*Well, this isn't creepy at all.*

Something moved to my far left, a muffled sound following.

"Farrah?"

My feet moved in that direction, stumbling to a halt when I saw her between the shelves.

She sat on the floor, her back to the wall,

seated amongst giant stuffed marine animals, a tortoise head resting on her knees.

I could just hear her whispered conversation, her crisp accent – a mix of upper-crust British from her youth and Astipian long vowels – danced through the air, a pleasant tingle starting in my scalp.

*Oh, shit.*

My eyes drifted shut as I strained to hear her. Not the words, her tone, the way she annunciated, the pop and crackle, the cadence and chorus of her voice.

My muse reared her head, stepping out from the cave she'd retreated into, dancing across Farrah's whispered voice, twisting Farrah's tone and using it to make beautiful music.

*I'm the cup to your saucer*
*You're the milk in my tea*
*Though the mist of tomorrow, I see you*
*And you see me.*
*You and your pretty eyes*
*Those wild highs*
*The nights we ran together, a surprise*
*Dance across my memories*
*It's you and me.*

My fingers itched for pen and paper, but all I had on me was my phone. I pulled it from my pocket, the words coming thick and fast as I listened to Farrah's voice, the soft tone more relaxing and inspiring than months of meditation had ever been.

*This fire between us burns a little higher*
*Like lava and the flame*
*This love cannot be tamed*
*You and me, girl*
*It's you and me.*

Farrah sighed, leaning back, falling silent.

My muse rebelled, tossing herself back into the cave she'd crawled from and slamming the door shut.

*Well, fuck.*

I tucked my phone in my pocket, realisation hitting me like a ton of bricks.

Farrah's voice had become the conduit for my muse.

"Fuck."

**5**

**Farrah**

"Fuck."

I startled, dropping the tortoise and banging my head against the brick wall behind me.

"Oh! Fuck!"

"Shit, Farrah, it's just me!"

Wolf materialised from behind a row of shelves, dropping to one knee before me, his hands reaching for my head.

"Let me see." He gently cupped my head, fingers running over the area where I'd cracked my skull against the wall.

He made a tutting noise, his face serious. "Definitely an intracranial bleed. I'm sorry, I'm gonna have to operate. Do you have a scalpel and some—"

I laughed, shoving him, setting him off balance and sending him tumbling to the floor. He grinned, tossing his shaggy hair away from his eyes.

My heart did a strange pitter-patter, memories simmering far too close to the surface.

"What are you doing back here?"

"Well...." He shoved up, sliding into place beside me, back to the wall, one shoulder and knee touching mine. "First, I wanted to say thank you for handling that woman."

I waved him off. "No thanks necessary. She was a bitch for filming you, but also, we have that policy for a reason."

His lips quirked into a smile. "Still, thank you."

"Second?" I asked, trying to shake off his praise even as my cheeks warmed.

"Second, I wanted to talk to you about the fundraising. I think—"

"Oh!" I twisted fully towards him, giving a little clap. "I came up with a solution!"

His mouth opened then snapped shut. "Sorry, what?"

"For the million dollars! I think I know how to raise it."

His face shuttered. "Go on."

"Actually, Anika – you remember my sister, right?"

He nodded.

"Well, she came up with it. We're going to host a fundraiser. Only, it's going to be a virtual one." Hope burned in my gut, fierce determination the only thing keeping me from breaking apart at this moment.

"She's friends with Laura Sweep and asked her for assistance. Laura loved the idea of a fundraiser and suggested we do carols by candlelight. Only this will be a virtual carols by candlelight charity event. People can log in to watch and will be prompted to donate to the Centre. We're going to host it on the twenty-second. She's already putting out calls to celebrities. They can do anything they want, sing, dance, make an omelette – the main thing is they just have to encourage people to donate."

I watched as Wolf scratched his chin.

"That's actually not a bad idea," he said slowly. "Celebs are gonna be feeling generous this time of year, and no massive overheads will mean all the money can be returned for profit."

I beamed, reaching out to catch his hand. "You started this, you know? I mentioned you to Anika, who mentioned you to Laura, and the next thing I know, she's calling me with this idea."

He looked down at our clasped fingers, his thumb grazing the back of my hand. Goose pimples rose at his innocent touch.

"How can I help?"

I froze, a sick feeling roiling in my belly. "Wolf, I can't ask you.... I mean.... you're on vacation."

He grinned, the smile reaching his eyes. "Farrah, that's why I want to. Because I know you didn't expect it of me. Let me help."

I swallowed, never too proud to accept help – not now when I needed a million dollars. "Okay."

"Will you get the money in time?"

"The bank said if we can prove we have the money coming, then they'll allow the extension I applied for. Which in turn will be enough to prove to the contractors that we're good to go for phase three."

He squeezed my hands. "That's awesome, Farrah. This is really good."

"Thanks." My cheeks flushed with his praise. "Laura and Liv, do you know Liv?"

He nodded, shuddering slightly. "That woman is crazy."

I laughed, nodding. "Yeah, Liv Larsson-Campbell is a little mental. But she's helping as well. All I have to do is record a few promos and speak about the Centre. They're bringing a crew this week to record the video."

"And that's why you're in this back room whispering to a stuffed turtle?"

I laughed, dipping my head to cover my embarrassment. "First, it's a tortoise and no, not quite. I just find saying things aloud helpful sometimes."

He nodded, dropping my hands to cross his arms over his chest, watching me with an inscrutable expression.

"What?"

Wolf hesitated, uncertainty creeping across his face. "I have a favour to ask."

"Anything."

"It's gonna sound weird."

I laughed, waving him off. "I doubt it."

"Could you record yourself whispering? I'll pay you for it."

I blinked. "Okay, I take that back. What!?"

**6**

**Wolf**

"Fuck." I ran a hand over my face. "Sorry, that came out wrong."

"Wrong? You want to pay me to whisper. How was it meant to sound?"

I blew out a breath, shaking my head. "I don't know... less creepy?"

She burst out laughing, her body hunching forward as she roared, the sound shaking something free from me.

*Tonight we'll laugh as the sun goes down*
*Shake up this year, light up this town*
*We'll dance till the sun relights the sky*
*While we toast to these endless days and unforgettable nights*

The lyrics hit me like a ton of bricks. I fumbled for my phone, fingers stuttering across the screen as I clumsily got the words down.

"What are you doing?" Farrah asked, shuffling closer.

"Writing lyrics." I glanced at her, a desperate need taking over. "Speak to me."

"What?"

"Please. Your voice it's..." I struggled to explain. "I'm inspired by sounds. When the sound feels good, it triggers my muse, and the words pour out."

"Feels good?" She tilted her head to one side, her mass of curls falling off her shoulder. "Explain?"

"Have you heard of ASMR?"

She shook her head, a little frown marring her brow.

"ASMR, autonomous sensory meridian response. It's when you get this pleasurable kind of tingling sensation in your body as a result of certain sounds. I'm probably botching this explanation. You can google it."

"So, it's a sex thing?"

I choked out a laugh, shaking my head. "No. Or at least it's not for me. It's more like... relaxation? Mediation? I'll hear a sound, and it'll feel pleasurable. I'll get tingles on my scalp or down my back, and I wanna hear it again. The more I hear it, the more I relax, and in that state, words come to me. I tend to include those sounds in songs, burying them into the mix so you wouldn't necessarily hear them, but I do. For my first album, I got inspired by the opening and closing of a bus door. I ended up riding around the metro all day just writing and listening to it. It's buried in Dark Love, if you're interested."

"Wow, that's actually kind of cool. Like a little easter egg." She tilted her head to one side, considering me. "Okay, I think I get it. It's like when a painter sees something they just need to capture. For you, it's sounds."

"Yeah, kinda."

Farrah pulled her feet into her chest, resting her chin on one knee. "And my voice does that to you?"

"Looks like it."

Her lips quirked. "I'm not sure if I should be flattered."

I rubbed sweaty palms down my jean legs. "Will you do it, though?"

"Whisper for you?"

"And laugh. Talk normally. Sing. Just do whatever feels comfortable."

"I... Did my voice always do this to you?"

I frowned, casting back, trying to remember.

*High school. Feeling calmer when Farrah was around. Her voice washing over me, setting my ten-*

*sion to rest. Her at Halloween this year, sitting around the fire, listening to her speak. Relaxing enough to remove my mask to hear her better.*

"Not to the point it does now where I'm starting to hear lyrics. But your voice has always generated a physical response in me."

Her face took on a weird expression, one I couldn't quite place.

"And you want to pay me for this?"

I nodded my heart in my throat.

*Say yes. I need this, Farrah.*

She blew out a breath, shaking her head. "I couldn't charge you. I'm happy to help."

"Then at least put me to work around the Centre. I can volunteer."

She laughed, stretching her legs out and beginning to stand. "That'd be a nightmare, you'd be mobbed in a moment. But if you really want to help, could you see if any artist friends would be willing to perform at our fundraiser? I know that's a huge ask, but I'd really appreciate it."

"Babe, of course." The endearment rolled off my tongue before I could stop it. Surprisingly, it felt right.

She paused, her eyebrows lifting slightly before she reached down, offering me a hand up. I took it, letting her haul me to a stand.

"So how do we do this?" She asked, our bodies close.

*Have I ever noticed that freckle before?*

I found myself distracted by the small details of her face. A faint freckle on her right nostril, the flecks of gold in her stunning eyes, the warm tone of her skin, the dark glint of her hair.

"Wolf?"

*Shit, pull it together, Rodriguez!*

"Um, stop by the studio tonight. We'll record you."

She blinked. "Studio?"

"It's at my house."

"Ah, the eco-lodge." She gave me an approving look.

I laughed, nodding. "You cool with that?"

"Would it be weird to admit I've been dying to get a look at your pipes?"

*Oh, I can show you some pipe.*

I cleared my throat, pushing away the strange thought.

*Farrah is a friend. A FRIEND. There is nothing sexual between us.*

*You sure about that?*

"Come by around six. I'll order some pizza; we'll do a cut. I'll give you a tour of the house."

Farrah smiled and something in me shifted, the world falling out from under me.

*Oh shit. I do like her.*

"Sounds good, I'll see you then."

She turned, heading towards the exit, leaving me standing like an idiot in their storage room, a stuffed giant turtle—no, tortoise—at my feet. I realisation dawned on me.

I loved Farrah.

I. Loved. Farrah.

*I love Farrah.*

*Well, fuck.*

7

## Farrah

I sucked in a breath, my fingers hovering over the keys of my ancient laptop. Down the hall I heard my roommate, Malik, whistling in the shower.

A notification dinged on my monitor.

YASMIN

Have you searched it yet?

FARRAH

No. I'm still too freaked out.

YASMIN

You have to do it soon. You're meant to be meeting him at 6!

My best friend was right. I needed to suck

this up and work out exactly what I was getting myself into.

I navigated to the google search bar.

WHAT IS ASMR?

Two-hundred and thirty million results.

*Oh, damn.*

There were videos, wiki pages, news articles and... medical journals?

I clicked one at random, a video opening.

"Hey, I'm Lucy, and I whisper for a living."

The next ten minutes were illuminating. ASMR wasn't some kind of kink (though it could be for some people) instead, it was exactly like what Wolf had described; a relaxed feeling in response to certain audio stimulations.

Not that I hadn't trusted him to be honest with me. I'd just worried he might not tell the *full* truth.

FARRAH

It's exactly like what he described.

YASMIN

!! Well that's good! Right?

My fingers flexed, some part of me aching.

FARRAH

Yeah.

YASMIN

Wait. You hesitated. Why did you
hesitate? DO YOU WANT IT TO
BE SEXUAL!?

I sat back pinching the bridge of my nose.

FARRAH

No. Maybe. I don't know. Wolf
is... Wolf.

YASMIN

So, hot as hell and totally crush-
worthy?

FARRAH

Ha ha. No... I mean yes. But... I
don't know. You know?

YASMIN

No. But yes. Why is this
confusing for you?

FARRAH

I honestly don't know. Maybe
because he's famous now?
And I'm...

"Broke. In debt. Struggling. Borderline un-
employable."

I scrubbed a hand over my face hating that I had these kinds of doubts.

YASMIN

If you were a mediocre white man in middle management would you have this thought?

I burst out laughing, shaking my head. Yasmin always knew how to cheer me up.

Malik knocked on my door.

"Farrah?"

"Come in."

He pushed it open, holding up his phone. "My sister text and said to tell you the following." He lifted his phone reading from the screen. "YOU ARE KICK ASS! YOU ARE A MOTHERFUCKING WOMAN! YOU DESERVE NOTHING BUT THE BEST!" He paused in his shouting. "Do you want me to read all the exclamation marks? 'Cause there are like fifty after that one."

I laughed, the weird ache dulling. "No, that's all good."

He leaned against the doorjamb. "Wanna talk about it?"

I hesitated. Malik and I were friends. We'd been thrown together thanks to me being best friends with his twin. He treated me as if I were just another sibling, and I did the same. There had never *ever* been a moment of sexual tension between us, despite what Yasmin may have wished. We were friends, and I loved that. He came to me for relationship advice, and while I'd never done the same, I knew I could if the need ever arose.

*I'd say the need has arisen.*

With a sigh, I slumped in my chair. "Wolf asked me over to his house."

Malik nodded, waiting for me to continue. When I didn't, he frowned.

"Wait? That's it?"

"I mean... kind of?"

I didn't want to tell him about the ASMR thing, not because Wolf would be ashamed, but more that it wasn't mine to tell.

"Okay, time for some reality-checking from your dear old roommate." He waggled a finger in my direction. "You are kick ass. You are a motherfucking woman. You deserve nothing but the best!"

I laughed, reaching out to snag a sock from my bed and throw it at him. "Get out!"

He grinned, shooting me a wink. "Seriously, Farrah, you're amazing. Wolf... he's missing something in his life. Something the fame took from him."

"What?"

"Connection." Malik sobered, his face darkening. "He no longer looks at people with trust. He looks at them and thinks, *what are they going to ask of me?* You? You're a known entity. You're the person he could trust."

"I already asked him for help," I admitted, regret tasting bitter on my tongue.

"Sure. But it's different, right? You asked him for help *with* something. Not *for* something. Did you ask him to pay off the debt?"

I shook my head.

"Exactly." He crossed to my seat, crouching to look me in the eye. "I know you like him. I know he likes you. You mighta thought I missed it, but I saw you both making out on Halloween."

My face flushed, the heat burning my cheeks. "You didn't squeal to your sister."

"Nah." he grinned. "I like having some secrets."

"What do you want?" I asked, knowing his silence would cost me.

He considered me, his lips pursing thoughtfully. "How about we call this one even?"

I cocked an eyebrow. "Excuse me?"

He shrugged, pushing back up and moving to leave my room. "Just love him right."

"I don't love him!" I protested to Malik's back.

"Sure. You keep telling yourself that."

"I'm serious! I don't love him!"

"Uh-huh! Totally believe you!" he called from down the hall.

I twisted back to my laptop, seeing Yasmin's final comment.

YASMIN

Look, I gotta go, Caleb is taking me out for dinner. But Farrah, just putting it out there, if you don't take a chance on love, you'll forever regret it. I love you. Now go get your man.

With a deep breath, I closed the laptop, looking out my bedroom window at the darkening sky.

*Get my man, hey? I guess I better dress for the job I want.*

My mobile buzzed, Yasmin texting me.

YASMIN

And wear the red dress. You know the one. You'll thank me later.

Gods bless best friends.

# 8

**Wolf**

*Oh, fuck.*

Farrah stood at my front door, her smile warm. Her riot of curls fell freely around her face and down her shoulders and back, her body encased in a short red Christmas dress complete with thigh-high candy cane socks. On her feet were cute boots. The red of her outfit set off the warm golden-brown tone of her skin, leaving me wondering if every inch of her looked so beautiful.

*Also, who am I that I'm noticing boots and calling them cute?*

*A man in love.*

I unstuck my tongue, desperately thinking of boring things in an attempt to quell my desire. Farrah was stirring feelings in me that I hadn't experienced in years.

"Come on in." I stepped aside, allowing her to squeeze past, subtly adjusting my hard as fuck cock while her back was to me.

*Calm the fuck down, Rodriguez. This is about the music, not your dick.*

With a firm mental slap to my face, I focused entirely on Farrah.

*Don't scare her off. Don't you fucking do anything to scare her off.*

"I thought we'd do the tour, maybe have some dinner, then head over to the studio – if that works?"

She nodded, her eyes wide as she took in the high ceilings and beautiful windows.

"Double glazed?" she asked softly, running fingers across the cool surface.

"Um, yeah."

*Two sides of the same mirror*
*But we never connect*
*You're left, and I'm right*
*Trying to bridge a gap needle thin*
*This is a battle neither can win*

"Shit, can you wait here a minute?" I dashed down the hall into my living space, crossing to the small side table where I'd tossed my notebook earlier. Flicking to a new page, I began to scribble the lyrics down.

I heard Farrah behind me, and I glanced her way. "Can you just... I don't know, just talk to me?"

A slight grin touched her lips, but she nodded, looking around the room. "What do you want me to talk about?"

I shrugged. "Anything. Your day, the weather. Anything."

She pursed her lips, a small frown marring her brow. "I had a below-average burger for lunch yesterday. I'm still struggling with the disappointment."

*Let down by the love that promised so much*

*We carve our hearts out but failed the life test*

*I'd give you the breath from my lungs, the blood from my veins*

*If only you'd do the same*

Words filled the page, notes and a melody taking shape.

My hand cramped, the ink in my pen running dry. I looked up, blinking when I registered the changes in the room.

When Farrah arrived, the sun had just been setting. I wasn't sure how long she'd been here, but the lights were switched on, the sky pitch black. A delicious smell hung in the air, Farrah chattering away as she bustled around my kitchen.

"—and then I asked if they wanted to help

me, and they all just laughed as if that were a strange question. I'm telling you, Wolf, you slip in bear poop once, and it's as if you're a social pariah forever."

"I'm sorry, did you say bear poo?"

The tongs Farrah had been holding fell to the floor with a loud clatter.

"Shit, sorry." I leapt up, springing over my couch and meeting her in the kitchen. She'd picked up the utensil, but sauce splatter decorated the kitchen cabinets and floor.

I pulled the cupboard above my fridge open, removing paper napkins to clean up.

"Shit, Farrah, I'm so sorry." I dropped to my knees, scrubbing at the splatter.

"Why are you sorry?" She asked, taking a wad of napkins. "I'm the one that dropped the tongs."

I blew out a breath, discarding the dirty napkins and reaching for new ones. "Sometimes I get in a...."

"A...?" Farrah prompted, leaning forward to clean another spot.

"A daze, I guess. It's hard to say exactly. It's like all I can see are the words, and all I can hear is the melody."

She rocked back on her heels, pressing a hand on her knee. "Wait, are you saying you didn't hear a word of what I said?"

I shook my head. "Not until my pen dried up."

"Huh." She tilted her head to the side, her eyebrows pulling together into a small frown. With a shake of her head, she leaned forward again, snatching up another napkin and crawling around, so her back was to me.

*Sweet mother of all that is holy...*

Farrah's ass was magnificent. As she bent over on all fours, I couldn't help but stare at her prime derriere, my cock hardening.

She wiggled, her body moving in time to her scrubbing.

*Jesus, Mary, and Freddie Mercury, grant me salvation from this torture.*

She rocked back, pushing to a stand and stretching her back a little. "Goddamn it, I'm getting old.

And just like that, I was transported back to Halloween night.

**9**

## Wolf

*Halloween night*

The Spiderman mask chaffed, but I ignored the discomfort, entirely too pleased to be out in public and not have been asked to pose for a selfie by a rabid fan even once.

*Best night of the year.*

We were sitting around the fire playing truth or dare. Malik and Hannah had disappeared off into the far corners of the yard, leaving my friend Caleb, Farrah, and Yasmin sitting around the fire.

"Truth or Dare, Spidey?" Farrah asked, her lips pursing, one eyebrow arched in my direction. That arch had me hardening, my cock begging for attention as her voice washed over me, generating pleasurable tingles.

*Fuck. It's been... shit. Five years. Five fucking years since I've made love to a woman. Fuck.*

Farrah Sharif looked like a goddamned dream. Hot as fuck in her steampunk assassin costume with that goddamned little top hat perched at a saucy angle. Every time she moved, it swayed, and I wanted to tear it from her head as I bent her against the side of the house, fucking her until we both came.

"Truth," I said, the words slightly muffled by the mask over my face.

She hesitated for a moment, and I tensed, knowing she was about to ask the question I didn't want to answer.

*Are you Wolf Rodriguez, world-famous singer and douchebag of the highest calibre?*

*That'd be an affirmative. Now, do you want one selfie or two? And how much will it cost me for you not to sell them to the press?*

"Who's better, Captain America or Iron Man?" Farrah asked, startling me.

A relieved chuckle slipped free as I leaned forward, elbows resting on my knees. "Captain America. Integrity, super speed. And he got his girl in the end."

Farrah's lips twitched, one side pulling up into a half-smile. "Okay, your turn."

And just like that, I knew she knew who I was. And for some reason, she didn't care.

*Well... this is an interesting turn of events.*

I turned away from her, considering the group, needing the out from the new feelings Farrah had stirred in me.

*It's gotta be the beer. And nostalgia. And the anonymity and...*

"Caleb, truth or dare?" I asked, looking at my friend.

"Go on then, dare." Caleb grinned, shooting Yasmin a wink.

Caleb Prince was a good friend, but the guy had zero clue when it came to women. He'd been in love with Yasmin since forever. And for some reason, she was the same.

*Maybe tonight it's time to give love a little push.*

"I dare you to spend seven minutes in heaven with Princess Jasmine over there."

Everyone froze, the fire crackling ominously in the wake of my dare.

Caleb coughed, clearing his throat, his voice hoarse as he asked, "sorry, what?"

I shrugged, enjoying this far more than I should. "Seven minutes in heaven. That's normally what people got dared to do back in the day, right?"

Caleb threw a look at Yasmin, who, dressed as Princess Jasmin, was staring back at him.

*Oh yeah, this is gonna either end with them together or with me being excommunicated by the town.*

Caleb shook his head. "Look, that's really a dare for both of us, and I don't want to make Yasmin—"

"Oh, come on." She handed her beer to Farrah, pushing up from her seat. "Seven minutes. I'll yell when you can start the timer."

She took Caleb's hand, pulling him along after her as she led him around the side of the house and into the shadows.

Which left me alone with Farrah.

I studied her for a moment as she stared at the shadows where Yasmin and Caleb had disappeared, a tiny smile playing on her lips. She caught me watching her, turning those big, brown eyes my way.

"You do realise they're in love with each other?"

I laughed, reaching for a beer from the tub beside me. "Doesn't everyone?"

"They don't."

"Well... maybe they will after tonight."

"You're evil," she said, her tone approving.

"Thanks."

I lifted a beer holding it out to her in a silent question.

"Sure."

She walked across the space, coming to sit beside me.

I handed the cool bottle off, pulling my mask up just enough to take a sip. It sat under my nose, reminiscent of the scene where Spiderman kissed Mary-Jane.

Farrah must have been thinking the same thing because her eyes locked onto my lips.

"You gonna keep that mask on all night?" she asked, her voice low and questioning. A lyric flittered in my brain, blinking for a moment, then fading away before I could snatch it.

"Is that a dare?" I asked.

"Hmm...." She took a long pull from her beer and then set it down. "Alright, truth or dare?"

"Dare."

"Take off the mask. Let me see your true identity."

I swallowed at the heat in her eyes. "Truth or dare, Farrah?"

She tilted her head to one side, her curls bouncing over her shoulder, that fucking hat tilting with her movement.

"Dare."

"I'll take it off. But you have to remove it for me."

The night took on a sultry feel, tension arching between us.

"Alright."

She closed the distance, and I opened my legs, silently inviting her to step between them.

"Where do you want me?" she asked, her voice low. The tingles in my scalp shot out, racing down my spine, setting nerve ends on fire.

"Sit on my thigh."

She did, perching on me, my hands coming up to hold her.

"Ready?" She asked, staring at the material covering my eyes.

"Go ahead."

Slowly, so slowly, she began to peel it up, revealing my skin in agonisingly minute detail.

She hesitated at my cheekbones, her fingers tickling my cheeks.

"What?"

"I need to do this first. Just so you know."

She leaned in, her lips pressing to mine, the mask barely concealing me. She tasted of cold beer and marshmallows, the combination intoxicating.

I deepened the kiss, my hands coming up to fist in her long curls, swallowing her muttered exclamation as I slipped my tongue between her lips.

I fucked her mouth with deliberate, delicious intent. I wanted to taste her. Wanted Farrah Sharif to sink into me and never let go.

A sound across the yard had her pulling back, her wide eyes staring at the shadows moving in the far corner.

"Malik," I whispered in warning, my body hard and aching. "You better move."

"In a second." She reached for the mask again, this time pulling it off in one easy move.

"Surprise," I whispered as her fingers caught in my hair.

"Wolf?"

"Mm?"

"Just so you know, as Spiderman or a rock star, I don't regret kissing you."

She retreated to her chair as Hannah and Malik returned to the fire.

"What did I miss?" Malik asked, plonking down into the seat beside me.

"Nothing," Farrah said, her gaze on me, a small secret smile on her lips. "Absolutely nothing at all."

**10**

**Farrah**

*Present day*

Oh. My. gods.
I froze, my gaze locked on the bulge in Wolf's pants.

*Cock. Dick. Big Cock. Huge. Ugh!*

My brain short-circuited, my body taking over.

Heat suffused every inch of my skin, a rhythmic pulse beating between my thighs. My legs clenched, my breasts heavy as my nipples responded in all their slutty glory.

*We're here! Come play with us!*

"You have a little..." Wolf reached out, his hand brushing my cheek. "Got it."

What I should have done was step forward and kiss him. I wanted to, oh brother, did I want to. But in a move I'd forever regret, I stepped back, my hands flying up to scrub at my face.

"How embarrassing!" I turned my back on him, busying myself at the counter. "Sorry, it's only simple butter chicken. You didn't have any garam masala, so it's not even technically butter chicken. More of a generic curry."

I babbled, tripping over my words as I tried to hide my embarrassment with words and food.

"Here." I picked up a plate, handing it to Wolf. "Dinner is served."

He looked down at the plate he suddenly found in his hands, his eyebrows knitting together. "You made this?"

"Sure, it's Dad's recipe. Minus the garam masala."

He looked up, grinning. "Is the garam masala essential?"

"Yes, but we'll deal."

Wolf placed his dish on the dining table and returned to the kitchen to bring out some wine.

"The least I can do since I've basically ignored you even while you made me dinner," he said as he cracked a bottle.

"Still not my worst date," I quipped, accepting the offered glass.

We chatted over the meal, following random threads and laughing far more than I had ever done on any other date.

*Not a date, Farrah. This isn't at all a date. This is work.*

"Your mom is British, right?"

"Yeah. Proper upper London," I replied, pushing my plate away with a happy sigh. "Dad and her met in Bali."

"He's a doctor?"

"Yeah. Left Mumbai to work for Doctors Without Borders. Mom researches turtles. They ended up in the same hostel, and the rest is history."

"Is she why you got into wildlife?"

I leaned back in my seat, swirling the wine around my glass, considering his question. "Both yes and no. Being around animals definitely influenced me. But, and this will sound strange, do you remember that field trip we took out to the Centre?"

He frowned. "We were, what? Grade six? Seven?"

"Something like that. We did a tour, and at the end, the woman asked for a volunteer. She chose me."

I laughed, remembering how excited I'd been. "She'd handed me a tortoise who had a cracked shell, explaining that he was traumatised and needed lots of love and care before he could be released. While she'd been speaking, he poked his little head out, checking me out."

I held up my right index finger. "Then he bit me, I bled everywhere, got a scar and fell in love with wildlife."

Wolf laughed, his eyes flashing with genuine amusement. "I remember that. The teacher was panicking, and you just said, 'it's a wild animal. What did you think it would do?'"

I chuckled, taking a sip of the rich wine.

He watched me over his own glass. "Did it sting not to get reelected?"

I sighed, shaking my head. "Yes and no. Being mayor was great. I got to help people, put our little town on the map, you know?"

"I sense a but."

"But," I agreed, grinning. "It took up an incredible amount of time and effort. And paid nothing. As in there was no money to pay me. Between that and the Centre... still, it sucked to lose to Carson."

Wolf grimaced. "Yeah, the guy is a douchebag."

"Gratifyingly, he doesn't strike me as competent, so I expect he'll be kicked out next election."

Wolf lifted his glass. "Now there's something I can toast to."

We clink glasses, both drinking deep.

"What about you? You could settle any-where in the world, and you came back."

He shrugged. "This is home. Some people might think it's too small or whatever, but this is where my dad met my mom. This is where they settled and raised a family. Nearly every memory I have of him is tied up here."

My heart ached. "You miss him."

"Every day. But the pain is less intense now. Mostly it just comes when I hit something I'd have called him about. Like graduating high school or making my first million."

I reached out, giving his hand a squeeze. "I only knew him a little, but I know he'd be proud of you."

Wolf grinned, the smile crooked but beauti-ful. "Yeah, I know."

We remained quiet for a little period after that, sipping our wine and watching the moon dance on the waves outside.

"Did you still want to record my voice?" I asked, liquid courage helping me raise the question.

Wolf paused. "Only if you're okay to do so?"

"Of course. That's what I'm here for, right?"

We cleaned up, the atmosphere shifting, becoming... more. More charged, more dy-namic, more...

*Sexual?*

It had to be a mistake, my hormones raging at being this close to such a charismatic and dynamic individual. Wolf sucked people into his orbit and kept them there with his wit and charm.

*Not to mention his looks.*

Oh yes, Wolf had a sexy nerd kind of look about him. Lean muscles, solid biceps, and a flop of dark hair that he constantly brushed from his face. When standing next to his brother, Tristan, one would know they were related from their faces, but their bodies were as different as night and day.

Wolf guided me through the house and out into the yard, both of us shivering in the cold night air.

"Snow?" I asked, looking up at the night sky.

"Maybe. It'd be cool to have a white Christmas."

"And yet you have no decorations?"

We made it to the studio, Wolf unlocking the door and gesturing me inside.

"That's because I'm in a standoff with my sister-in-law."

"Honey?" I asked, looking around at the lit space. "Doesn't she love decorating?"

"Oh, yeah. She's gonna crack any day now,

and I'll come home to a full winter won-
derland."

"You do realise you're essentially torturing
her into free labour?"

"Yep. But she's asked me to come over next
week and make muffins. Something about a
holiday bake sale to raise money for the
precinct. I'll also take Nicole for a weekend, so
my brother and her can get some *alone* time."

I giggled, watching as he pressed buttons
and twisted dials on the sound desk.

"Okay." He led me through the studio to the
recording area, gesturing for me to take a seat at
the microphone.

I did, watching as he walked around, plug-
ging things in and switching things on. He came
back a moment later, holding up some giant
earphones.

"All you need to do is speak into this." He
gently tapped a finger on the microphone. "I'll
be listening on the other side. You'll hear me
through the earphones."

I nodded, wiggling slightly on my seat, my
knee jiggling nervously.

"You cool if I pop these on you?"

I nodded again, lifting my head as Wolf
leaned over, gently tucking the curls on either
side of my face behind my ears. Satisfied, he
slid the earphones over my ears, double-

checking the fit and adjusting them before stepping back.

*Stay there,* he mouthed, gesturing at me to remain seated as he left the booth. I waited, watching anxiously as he appeared on the other side of the glass at the sound desk.

"Okay, let's test some levels. Start talking for me."

"About?" I asked, my hands lifting to touch the ear coverings.

"Anything. The weather, the book you're reading, what you want for Christmas."

*You.*

I shoved the rogue thought away. "Well, that's easy, I want this fundraiser to be a success."

"Are you performing?"

I blinked. "What?"

Wolf paused, looking up from his tinkering. "You do know you're an amazing singer, right?"

I shook my head slowly.

"Farrah..." he paused, twisting to pull something up. "Do me a favour and sing this."

Music filtered through the earphones; the opening notes familiar.

"Wolf..."

"Just trust me."

I sucked in a breath, closed my eyes and began to sing Elton John's Your Song.

At the end, the music looped, Wolf's voice coming through the earphones.

"Go again, and this time lean into it. It's just you and me, Farrah."

I opened my eyes, catching his gaze. He had a pen in one hand, the expression he'd worn earlier tonight as I'd chattered at him back in place.

"Wolf...?"

He shot me a grin. "Just sing, babe. Please."

So, I did, my eyes glued to him, spellbound by his enjoyment. As I sang, he seemed to lose himself, his eyes closing and his hands coming up to pluck the strings of an imaginary guitar. As I reached the bridge, he began to madly scribble across the pages of a notebook, his head bopping in time to a beat only he could hear.

*This is the weirdest and best experience of my life.*

I didn't know how to describe this moment. Perhaps I should be insulted that he spaced out when I spoke or sang, but instead, I found myself strangely flattered.

The song finished, and silence dominated the space, Wolf lost to the music only he could hear.

I found myself watching him, content to

simply be in the same space. A frown marred his forehead, his pen slowing.

I licked my lips, deciding to take a chance.

"Once upon a time, a girl lived in a castle."

I watched as the frown eased from Wolf's face, his pen picking up pace, his hand flying across the page.

"The young girl lived within the high walls, her only view that of the sky. Sun, clouds and rainbows, stars, comets and the moon, her only friends." I grinned as Wolf pushed away from the desk, beginning to pace as he continued to write.

"One day, a crow crashed in the courtyard, her wing broken.

'What are you?' the girl asked.

'I'm a crow,' replied the crow. 'Can you help mend my wing?'

The girl agreed, and they became fast friends."

Wolf stopped, his head tilting to one side as listening.

"One day, the crow woke, realising that her wing had healed.

'I must go,' said the crow to the girl. 'For crows aren't meant for cages in castles.'

'But what about me?' asked the girl.

'You can come too. But first, you must break down these walls.'

The girl, having never noticed the walls before, looked around in surprise. 'You mean this isn't the world?'

'You mean to think it is?' replied the crow.

With courage and might, the girl began to dismantle the walls one stone at a time until nothing stood between her and the world.

'It's big,' said the girl.

'And scary. And wonderful. And ready for you,' said the crow. 'If only you'll take the first step.'

With a deep breath and open heart, the girl walked into the world having rescued herself. The end."

Wolf's head jerked up, his gaze snapping to me, focusing in on me. "Hey, where'd you hear that?"

"I'm surprised you heard all that," I said with a laugh.

He grinned. "I'm writing, not deaf. It's like... I still hear the words, but they process in and out." He held up the notebook. "And thanks to the story, I've got a new song."

"That's cool, did you need me to—" I cut off as he move out of view. A moment later, he entered the recording room, carrying the notebook and a small stool.

"Okay, here are the lyrics." He handed me

the notebook, pointing at the page. "Follow my lead, I'll guide you through as we go."

"Wait, what?" I shook my head. "Wolf, I can't—"

"Come on, Farrah. This is the song you helped write."

I looked down at the page as Wolf bustled about setting himself up on the stool beside me. He plugged his acoustic guitar in, settling a spare pair of earphones over his ears.

"Ready?" he asked, plucking strings.

"No, not at all." My pulse kicked up, anxiety cramping my stomach.

He grinned. "You'll be perfect. Just follow me."

And with that, he began to strum.

**11**

**Wolf**

Farrah had the kind of voice that record companies killed to sign, and this song would only work with a female singing it.

*She's gonna be a millionaire before Christmas next year.*

"Okay, I'm gonna do an intro, then give you the nod. Just see how it feels. No pressure."

Farrah nodded, the notebook trembling in her hands as I transitioned from general strumming to the opening melody, the notes already embedded in my mind.

I gave her a nod, watching as she opened her mouth, the beauty of her unfurling as she gave herself into the music.

"Some castles are golden cages with walls
princesses can't climb
    They're built by men with smiling faces
    Who keep us trapped inside
    They built them with pieces
    Chipped from our broken souls
    They say it keeps the monsters out
    But those are lies, they're already here


GIRL, embrace the flame
    Scale the walls and break them down again
    Pick up the pieces of you
    And forge yourself back together
    Back together, back together 'til whole
    You're a force to be reckoned with
    A storm no one can contain
    A general on a battlefield
    Girl, embrace the flame


WALLS MAY LOOK insurmountable
    And you don't know where to start
    We all gotta begin where we are
    There's a power, there's a spark
    Its hidden in you
    And hidden in me
    Don't contain or bury it deep
    Let it explode into a million pieces

*Scatter to the four ends of the earth*
*Let us crush these walls into dust beneath your*
*fingers tips*
*Grind these walls into dust beneath your fin-*
*gertips*
*Girl, embrace the flame*


SCALE THE WALLS *and break them down again*
*Pick up the pieces of you*
*And forge yourself back together*
*Back together, back together 'til whole*
*You're a force to be reckoned with*
*A storm no one can contain*
*A general on a battlefield*
*Girl, embrace the flame*


GIRL, *embrace the flame*
*Girl, embrace your flame*
*Embrace your flame*
*And let's set the world on fire."*

Farrah sat back, her gaze on me as I finished with a final flourish, holding my hand up for a high-five. She slapped my palm, her expression a mix of joy and stunned surprise.

"Wolf... that's...." She shook her head, laughter spilling free. "Amazing! Honestly, that song is everything. It's like you reached into here—" she touched her chest, "—and pulled out everything I feel."

I waved off her praise. "Let's run through a few takes then, I wanna hear how it sounds."

She nodded, moving back into position. "Any notes?"

"Nope, just go with the flow."

We recorded well into the night until I finally called it around 2am.

"Alright, should we listen?"

She nodded, her eyes glinting, hyped up on adrenaline.

We exited the booth, making our way to the sound desk. I slid into a chair, gesturing at Farrah to sit as my fingers ran over the desk.

"Has it been recording this whole time?"

"Uh-huh," I muttered, checking the levels and quickly scoping which recording looked to be the best.

Farrah sat down beside me, reaching for the small bar fridge under the sound desk. Inside were soft drinks, some chocolate bars, fruit and bottles of water.

She pulled one out, handing it to me. I took it absently, focused on what the computer was telling me.

"Okay, here we go."

I made a final adjustment and then hit play.

The guitar started strong, already plucking

at the heartstrings, encouraging you to be better, to be more.

"Some castles are golden cages with walls princesses can't climb..."

Farrah started, her gaze flying to meet mine. Her eyes danced with excitement; her cheeks flushed with pleasure.

*She's gonna be a star.*

We sat like that for the full three minutes and twenty-two seconds, our eyes locked as her voice and my guitar washed over us, calling us to set the world on fire. Silence descended, both of us still locked in the magic.

"Wolf...."

I leaned forward, catching the back of her neck in my hand, pulling her towards me.

Our lips met in a mash of gasps and hungry grunts. Desire mixed with adrenaline, my body humming with need.

"Fuck, Farrah!" I hauled her into my lap, fisting her curls and tilting her head to give me better access. Gratifyingly, Farrah wrapped herself around me, giving over, a whimper working its way up her throat, the sound generating new lyrics.

*Hard and hot*
*Nights together*
*Kisses stolen beneath shadowed doors*

*Our lips touch as we swear promises over cheap beer and red wine*
*You taste like sin*
*You feel like heaven*
*Call me a disciple*
*You're my religion*

My cock lay hard and hot, rigid as fuck, as Farrah bore down on me, her body crying out for more delicious friction.

*Oh gods. Fuck. Fuck.*

"Wolf!" Her voice cut through my desire, refocusing me.

*It's been over five years, don't let this end before it's even begun.*

My hands cupped her ass through her dress, my tongue dancing with hers as I ground up against her core, nerve endings tingling in the most delicious way.

*Don't come, don't come, don't come!*

I'd had years of sexual experiences, and not one came even close to the intensity of this moment. No disrespect to the other women, we'd had fun. But with Farrah? Love made all the difference.

*And I'm sure the five-year hiatus is also contributing.*

"Need to...." I dropped both hands to her beautiful thighs, sliding them up and under her dress, rearing back as I encountered more bare skin. "Farrah, what the fuck?"

She gasped against my mouth as my calloused fingers dug into the cheeks of her butt. "This dress shows panty lines."

"Jesus, Mary, and Jon Bon Jovi!" I swore, shoving up her dress, needing to see her body. Curls at the junction of her thighs, her warm brown skin flushed with arousal. I pushed the fabric higher, practically panting at the yards of gorgeous skin I revealed.

And then I hit the motherload, her lace-encased breasts.

"Fuck..." I groaned, yanking the dress over her head and tossing it to the side. "You're killing me, Sharif."

With a husky laugh, she arched her back, cupping the small mounds and offering her breasts to me. "You mean these?"

I slid greedy hands under the cups, pushing the lace up until her dusky nipples were revealed.

"I'm gonna fuck these breasts," I promised, the filthy fantasy slipping free before I could stop it. "Gonna come all over your tits, your neck, your face."

She arched an eyebrow, a small smile playing at the corners of her mouth. "And if I say no?"

I swallowed, reigning myself in. "I'll respect your wishes. This is a partnership, Farrah, everything we do isn't gonna float each other's boat. We just need to be open about it."

"Correct answer." She leaned back, placing her hands on my knees behind her, her breasts pushed forward, close enough to taste. "Have at it, Wolf."

With a strangled curse, I leaned forward, capturing her nipple in my mouth, moaning at the taste. I teased the bud of one breast, my tongue circling, mouth sucking greedily. Farrah's fingernails dug into my skin, her body shuddering as my hand came up to palm her other breast, teasing and pinching, soothing and building her need with every touch.

I could feel her heat against the crotch of my jeans, her body taking up a sensual grind as the scent of her arousal hit me.

*Fuck. Yes.*

With a growl, I picked her up, carrying her across the room to the couch. I laid her down, spreading her legs, my fingers dancing through her wet heat.

"You're a naughty girl," I praised, my tone rough. "You want me to fuck you here, don't you?"

She whimpered, reaching out to thread fingers through my hair. I curled a finger, pressing my knuckle to her clit, slowly rubbing, finding her rhythm.

"I need words, Farrah."

"Yes!" She cried, my fingers dancing along her little clit. "I need you. I want you in me. I need your cock to fuck me. Please, Wolf."

Her desperation broke what little restraint I had left. In one move, I pulled my sweater and shirt over my head, tossing them to the side. I fumbled at my jeans, Farrah crunching up to help me. With desperate hands and hot kisses, we shoved down my pants, both of us tasting any inch of skin within reach.

"Hurry up!" She grunted, wiggling under me.

"I don't want to—" I choked off, my eyes rolling into the back of my head as she fisted my cock, giving it a rough jerk.

"In me. Now!"

"You are a motherfucking goddess, and I love you."

With wild eyes and fierce hair, Farrah guided me to her, her hand dropping away as I fucked up, thrusting hard and taking her fast.

*Tight. Hot. Wet. Tight. So, fucking tight.*

She whimpered, her body clenching under me, a painful expression crossing her face.

"Farrah?"

"Sorry, I just... I've only ever done this by myself."

"You... wait. What does that mean?"

She gave me a crooked smile. "I guess, technically, I'm still a virgin. Though my toy collection would have you thinking otherwise."

And with that admission, my brain exploded.

**12**

**Farrah**

I couldn't be a hundred percent sure, but I think I'd just blown Wolf's mind.

I gave an experimental wiggle, relieved to find only a slight discomfort which was quickly overtaken by pleasure.

"Oh, umm... you can move now." I told him, my fingers cupping his butt and giving him a little encouraging pull in my direction.

"Sorry, I'm... You're... A virgin?" He asked, giving me slow blinks.

"Former," I said, gesturing between us. "Now, can we...?"

He seemed to shake it off, the hungry, possessive expression returning. "Oh, we definitely can."

He dropped his head, licking his way between my breasts, laving at one and then the other. One hand kept him braced above me, the other snaking between our bodies to glide through my wet curls, finding my clit.

"Here's the deal. We're gonna get you off at least twice, then I'm gonna come in you. We'll head back to the house, where I'll eat you out and fuck your sweet breasts until I come. After, we'll clean up in the shower, where I'll inevitably need to go down on you again. Once done, we'll go to bed, sleep for a few hours then start over again. Sound good?"

My body, already primed, melted, trembling around him.

"Um... yes?"

His grin was pure male satisfaction.

"Great." He pressed a finger against my clit, rubbing gently. "And for the record? I'm clear. Five years of abstinence, fuck, I'm practically a born-again virgin." He leaned in, nipping at my collarbone, the scruff of his chin grazing my skin. "Be gentle with me?"

I chuckled, the movement of my body setting nerve endings tingling. "I'm also on the pill, so we should be good."

"Thank Christ."

And with that conversation done, he leaned in, kissing the fuck outta me as his hands did wonderfully wicked things to my body.

"Farrah," he murmured as his body moved against mine, his cock filling me in the most delicious of ways.

Wolf made love to me and even being a virgin, I could tell the difference. He cared for my body, learning it, paying avid attention to my gasps and shudders, seeking what gave me pleasure and learning what didn't.

"Oh gods," I groaned, my eyes closing as I began to ride the tide of pleasure. "I'm gonna—" I broke off with a strangled cry, my body shattering into a million pieces as I came.

"Fuck yes, that's it, babe." Wolf's gruff encouragement tipped me over, sending me spiralling higher.

I came back to myself with an abrupt thud as the door to the studio smashed open, Wolf's bodyguards bursting through, tasers at the ready.

"What the fuck?" Wolf roared, covering me with his body, his cock still hard as a rock inside me. "Get the fuck out!"

The men, assessing the situation, spun on their heels, their backs turned to us.

"Shit, sorry." The one on the right barked. "We did rounds, and you weren't in bed and hadn't flagged where you were, so we thought...."

Realisation slammed into me.

*Wolf isn't your high school crush. Wolf is a famous rock star.*

I pushed at his chest, forcing us apart. He slid free, his cock rigid and heavy. I took a second to glance at it, appreciating both the length and heft before my mortification crowded in.

I scrambled for my dress, tugging it on sans underwear. I abandoned my bra, grateful I still wore my socks, my boots having been discarded beside the door hours before. I scooped them up, snagged my purse from beside them and head for the door – a door in which two hefty blokes currently stood.

"Excuse me, sorry, excuse me."

"Farrah, wait. I—"

I waved Wolf off, dodging his outstretched hand. He'd pulled on jeans, the undone fly revealing the soft patch of hair at his abdomen. I tried not to notice.

"I gotta go, I'll call you!" I promised, my voice high-pitched and breathy. "Thanks for a lovely evening! Good night!"

With a quick spin, I snaked between the two men, practically sprinting for the exit.

"Farrah!"

I stumbled through the door, hurrying across the yard and making it to my car as Wolf came outside, his chest bare, the jeans still low on his hips.

"Farrah!"

"Bye!"

I put the car in gear, attempting to thread my seatbelt over my chest as I took off. In the rear vision mirror, I caught sight of Wolf standing in the courtyard, his face stricken as the first little flakes of snow began to fall from the sky.

*Gods damn it all.*

**13**

**Farrah**

"Wait. You just *left*?" Yasmin stared at me as I slumped on my chair, wishing I could sink under the table. "Oh, Farrah."

We'd met for brunch at my sisters' bar. Anika let me eat for free if I cleaned her house once a week.

Yasmin had answered my SOS. She'd arrived, took one look at my face and wrapped me in a hug while ordering me to spill my woes. It'd been two days since I'd seen Wolf, and I had no idea whether I was relieved or annoyed by this fact.

*Liar. You're upset. You want to see him. You lov—*

"I know," I cried, dropping my head on the table and bumping it against the surface. "I'm an idiot."

"Well, I wouldn't say that just..." Yasmin glanced around, biting her lip. "But it's not great, Farz."

I sighed heavily, mentally beating myself up. "I know."

"You're going to have to talk to him. Wolf's one of the lead acts at the fundraiser on Wednesday, you can't just ignore the guy."

"I know." I sighed again into the tabletop, bumping my head once more before lifting to stare at my best friend. "I'm just so embarrassed. Yazzy, I practically forced him. He's a world-famous rock star, and I'm... no one. Hell, I'm in debt! I don't even have ten dollars to my name. I live in a share house with your brother because I can't afford my own apartment. Last week I ate peanut butter sandwiches for every meal to afford rent." I sucked in a breath, fighting tears. "I feel like such a fool."

"Okay, you need to stop." Yasmin held up a hand, her delicate fingers straight and firm. "This pity party is getting out of hand, and I will *not* allow you to talk to my friend that way." She leaned in, her eyes glinting with anger. "You are amazing. You are beautiful. You are selfless, Farrah. You, my friend, are totally above any rock stars. You are in a league of your own, and how *dare* you question your amazingness. Pull yourself together, woman up, and go talk to this guy. You let him into your body, now let him into your heart."

I sucked in a breath, simultaneously pissed off at her and overwhelmed with love.

"I hate you," I said without heat.

"I know." She reached for a sugar packet, throwing it at me. "Now go get your man."

I nodded, straightening my back and squaring my shoulders. "Yeah. Yeah, you're right. I'm gonna go right now and—"

A waiter slid a plate of steaming waffles in front of me, placing a small pot of chocolate sauce on the side.

"—eat this breakfast first, then head over." I amended, reaching for my fork.

"Sounds like a plan," Yasmin agreed, lifting her own fork to spear a slither of bacon on her plate.

I leaned forward, already feeling lighter. "Now, can I fill you in on Malik and his mystery woman?"

"Oh, please do. Anything I can use to torture my brother over Christmas dinner is most welcome."

I HOVERED outside the gate to Wolf's property, attempting to psych myself up.

*You can do this. It's not that hard. Honestly, all you need to do is press the buzzer. Come on, girl! Be strong!*

I reached out, pressing the button.

"Name and appointment?" The voice asked.

"Um, hi. I'm Farrah. I—"

"Come on up."

The gate buzzed, sliding open. I pushed my bike through the gap, heading up the frozen drive to the house.

With so much to do over the next few days, I found myself needing to ration my car's fuel to make it through. It sucked, but riding every-where was healthy for you – or so I reminded myself as my breath misted in front of my numb face.

At the house, a man stood in the entry, arms crossed, expression stern.

"Farrah?" he asked, watching me park my bike.

"Yeah?"

He held out a hand. "I'm Omar. Alec and I were there the other night. We just wanna say sorry."

My blush was sudden and severe. "Oh, um... thanks."

He dropped my hand, still not yet inviting me in.

"Wolf's upstairs with his agent. And... Farrah? I gotta tell you, the boy is broken up over you. So, if you're here to do anything other than try to make this work, then I'd kindly ask you to leave."

"I can promise you I'm not here to hurt him. But whatever is between us is between *us*."

He considered me for a long moment, his gaze sweeping my face before he gave a single nod. "Okay. That's fair. Come on through."

I headed upstairs, pulling my gloves off one at a time, trying not to blush as I remembered the last time I'd been here.

*Talking for Wolf while he wrote beautiful mu-sic. Eating with Wolf. Laughing with Wolf. Making love with Wolf.*

I found him in the lounge, a fire crackling merrily in the hearth. Wolf caught sight of me, his gorgeous eyes widening. He stood abruptly, papers falling from his lap.

"Farrah?"

"Hey." I lifted a hand, offering a stupid little wave. "Is now a good time?"

Wolf stared at me, that endearing flop of hair covering his forehead.

"I'd say you're right on time, young lady." The gentleman with Wolf rose, buttoning his suit jacket and walking across to shake my hand. "Allow me to introduce myself, I'm Glenn Burnes. I represent Wolf and, I hope, you."

I took his hand on autopilot, my mouth opening to introduce myself when my brain stuttered to a halt over his comment. "Ex-ex-cuse me?"

He grinned, dropping my hand and sweeping an arm out towards the lounge chairs. "Come and sit. We have a lot to discuss."

Wolf remained silent as Glenn and I took seats across from him. Wolf reminded me of his namesake as his hungry gaze swept over me.

"Now tell me, Farrah, what are your plans for the next twelve months?"

I stumbled over my words, confused by his question. "I... I don't know. Hopefully, finalising the new project build at the Wildlife Centre. Maybe training some new staff."

*Making love with Wolf to celebrate our first anniversary together.*

Glenn nodded, knitting his fingers together and bringing his joined hands to his mouth. "What if I told you that you'll be a millionaire and getting ready to headline the New Year's Eve Ball Drop?"

I laughed, amusement wrapping itself around me and breaking the tension of this moment. "I'd say could I have that million dollars tomorrow?"

"Yes," Wolf replied, his face deadly serious. "Farrah, you're gonna be famous."

I frowned. "I'm sorry?"

Glenn lifted his phone and tapped the screen. A beat later, my voice filled the space, piping out of the hidden speakers as I sang Wolf's song.

He let it play for a moment before hitting pause, silencing the music.

"I... I don't understand." I looked from Wolf to Glenn. "What's happening right now?"

"I want to sign you and release this single. Wolf has written you an album—" Glenn swung a hand out, encompassing the piles of papers strewn over the coffee table and sofa. "—and I'm prepared to take you on as a client, provided you get formal legal advice before signing with me."

I swallowed, my stomach clenching, my mouth bone dry. "I don't understand. I really don't."

Glenn leaned forward, capturing one of my hands. "Farrah, your voice is special, and you have a choice. Take the gift offered to you or reject it. This doofus—" he flicked a finger towards Wolf, "—has added your name to every single one of these songs. So, either we make you a singer, or you remain co-writer of this album, and I sell these to some other young diva. Either way, it's your choice."

My mind reeled, my body tight. Tears burned the back of my lids, my mouth dry, my stomach a clenched ball of nervous energy.

"Wolf, what have you done?" I whispered, my voice breaking.

"Shit." He stalked across the small gap, scooping me up and lifting me into his arms. "We'll be back."

With that, he carried me down the hall, kicking the door to his bedroom shut and placing me gently on the edge of his massive bed.

I clung to him, my world adrift and sinking fast.

"Wolf, I don't understand what's going on."

He pushed away from the bed, beginning to pace.

"Wolf? Speak to me."

"You have a talent, Farrah. I heard it in high school, I heard it when we messed around on Halloween night, and I heard it again when we recorded your first single. You could be the next hit sensation, rocketing up the charts, smashing records. You deserve that."

"But what if I don't want it? Wolf, you're making these decisions without even asking."

He shook his head. "I know you love the Centre, but think of the good you could do. As someone with a public platform, you have an opportunity to educate people. One endorsement from you and millions will know about your work."

I sucked in a breath, imagining the dream he painted.

*Money to expand the Centre. Money to hire more staff. Money to buy more land and save more animals.*

My ever-practical brain intruded, reminding me of the practicalities of Wolf's life.

*No privacy. Bodyguards. Tours. No time to actually be at the Centre.*

*No Wolf.*

"What about us?" I whispered, my voice breaking. "What happens with us?"

He froze, his body stiffening. "Is there an us?"

I rose, cupping his cheek. "I thought there was."

His hand came up, pressing mine against his skin, his dark eyes searching my face. "Even after the other night?"

I quirked a smile. "I mean, I won't be retelling that one often but it'd nice to finish what we started. And maybe redo it a million or so times."

"Farrah... I want you to have everything you deserve." He swallowed. "Fame has a cost, as you know. But you deserve to have the opportunity to explore who you are. If you still want me then we'll make it work."

"I know. And I get it. But Wolf, I'm happy here. I don't need fame and fortune. I need purpose. Joy. Love."

His cheek jumped under my hand, his eyes shadowing. "What does that mean?"

I grinned, my body feeling lighter. "I love singing with you, Wolf. But its not the same for me as it is for you. When you sing or write or perform it's a joyful moment. For me it's nothing but anxiety and fearing I'll stuff up. I don't feel that way working with the animals. Even knowing I need a million dollars doesn't make this a tempting offer. I am who I am, Wolf. And who I am is an activist."

For a moment he seemed about to protest, his mouth opening, his face scrunching into a frowning. Then it all faded, tension in his body drifting away.

"You're serious."

"Deadly," I agreed.

"I have a confession to make, but first I need to ask you something."

"Okay...."

He sucked in a breath. "Can you take a

chance on us? I know it's a lot to ask. You'll get threats from women, have your looks picked apart, you'll probably end up with a crazy stalker or two. I'll need to assign you a body-guard, and I'll want you to come on tour with me sometimes even though tours are shit hard and I'll have hardly any time to give you."

I grinned, sinking into him. "I don't know, that depends."

His body remained tight and tense under mine. "On?"

I lifted onto my tiptoes, leaning forward until my mouth was close to his ear. "Are you going to let me whisper naughty things to you?"

He shuddered a whole-body tremble that went from the top of his head to the tips of his toes. Delighted, I leaned more heavily into him, lowering my voice even further, gratified by the feel of his cock as it began to harden against my stomach.

"Cause I want to explore this ASMR thing a little more. I want to see if it brings out just words or if it'll inspire you in the bedroom. I wanna see if I can make you come just by—"

He cut me off with a swift kiss, his mouth forging to mine, his hips rocking into me, pressing his hard member to my stomach.

"Yes, to everything," he groaned against my mouth. "You filthy deviant."

Giggles burst free as I jumped up, wrapping myself around him, Wolf's hands automatically catching me and holding me close.

"Wait." I pulled back, halting our kiss. "What was the second thing?"

"What?" he asked, his hair dishevelled, his gaze glazed with desire.

"You said you needed to make a confession."

"Fuck, yeah, I do." His hands spasmed on my ass, his body tensing once more. "Farrah, I need you to know I love you."

I melted against him.

"I love you so much. You're my muse. You give me the breath in my lungs. On Halloween, I wrote the first song I'd written in over twelve months. After that, nothing. Then we reconnected, and it's like you've tapped something inside me. I listen to you speak, I hear your voice, I touch you, and my muse goes into overdrive. I've written a seventeen-song album. I'm working on a dozen more. Writing each one reminds me of you. I don't know when it started or how it happened, but you're it for me."

I tilted my face back, ready for him to claim me.

"Which is why what I have to say is so hard."

My heart stuttered, fear shivering up my back. "Oh, gods. Just tell me."

He closed his eyes for a moment, then

opened them, pegging me in place. "Farah, I donated five million to the Centre. I know you'll be angry, but let me explain. First, it's a great tax write-off and..."

Wolf's voice faded into white noise, my eyes locked on his face as he continued to speak, justifying his decision.

*Five million dollars.*

*Five. Million. Dollars.*

*Five.*

*Million.*

*Dollars.*

"Farrah?"

The worry, frustration, fear, all of it broke over me, shattering my control. Tears burst free, my body heaving as I sobbed, relief the sweetest taste in the world.

*I'm going to marry this man.*

**14**

**Wolf**

Farrah thrust her face in my neck, her body wracked with sobs.

*Oh fuck.*

Panic clawed up my throat, fear that I'd just fucked up far worse I'd ever done before.

*Seriously dude, first the coitus interruptus, then the singing, and now this? You're fucking this up before it begins.*

> Before you beat yourself up
> some more, maybe ask her
> opinion? I love you, son. Make
> me proud.

My dad soothed me, his sound advice cutting through the clutter in my head. With

Farrah in my arms, I pivoted, dropping to sit on the edge of the bed, Farrah wrapped around me like a baby Koala.

"Talk to me, babe."

She looked up, her eyes red, her nose dripping, her cheeks flushed and swollen. I'd never seen a more beautiful woman in my life.

"We're naming the Centre after you," she declared with a determined sniff. "Or if you want to call it the Rodriguez Rescues for Turtley Turtles, I don't care." She pressed a quick kiss to my lips. "Wolf, you've changed my life. You've changed the lives of everyone who works or will work at the Centre. Do you even understand how many animals you've saved? And now I can pay a living wage to my staff. You've given me breathing space where before I was drowning. You say I give you the breath in your lungs? Wolf, you are the air in mine. I've, creepily, loved you since high school. I love you now. I love everything about you, and I can't wait to love everything you reveal to me in the future."

"So, you're not angry?" I asked as she peppered kisses across my face.

"Fuck no." She pulled back, cupping my cheeks. "I've been screwed over by so many people. And yes, it probably makes me selfish to not even protest a little, but I don't have it in me.

You've lifted the weight off my shoulders. Thank you."

I brushed off her thanks, uncomfortable with the praise. "I don't want it named after me. That's weird. All I did was donate some cash."

She tilted her head to one side, her lips pressing together in thought. "What if we named it after your dad?"

My heart leapt into my throat; my eyes suddenly itchy.

How about it, Dad? I suspect you'd get a kick out of that.

For the first time, his voice didn't answer, and I somehow knew it was unlikely I'd ever hear him again. I had Farrah now.

Goodbye, Dad. I love you.

I focused on my woman, needing to clear my throat before I could answer.

"I'd love that," I admitted, lifting her hand to press a kiss to her knuckles. "And I know Mom would too."

"Done." She brushed a thumb over my cheek. "I love you, Wolf."

"And I love you, Farrah."

"Make love to me?"

Her sweetly utter question ignited a fire in my blood. "Fuck yes."

I kissed her collarbone, my lips caressing her skin as I tasted her sweet spots. Under me, she sighed, her eyelids drifting close, her body sinking deeper into mine.

I kissed up her neck, finding sensitive spots on the underside of her jaw, the skin behind her ear, and the tip of her earlobe. With infinite patience, I slowly kissed my way to her mouth, devouring it with a single-minded purpose.

We stripped each other, hands fumbling and bumping, laughter always on the tips of our tongues.

"Wait," Farrah pushed me back a fraction, her shirt having been discarded on the floor, her pants half undone. "I wanna do something."

She slid down my body, falling to her knees beside the bed, her fingers deftly undoing my fly.

"What are you—" I choked off my question as her hand wrapped around my cock, her mouth following. "Farrah!"

She chuckled, the vibration against my length near unbearable as her deliciously hot mouth began to work my cock, her tongue teasing my shaft, her fingers working my root.

*Ducks and geese, peg the seagull. A hedgehog. Paparazzi.*

I conjured desperately, seeking any fleeting thought that might save me from embarrassing myself by spilling too quickly in her mouth.

"Farrah, stop!"

She paused, my cock pulsing in the hot heat of her mouth.

"I'm too on edge. I need to taste you."

She sighed, closing her eyes and slowly easing off my cock. "Go on then. If you must, I suppose I can suffer through it."

I chuckled as I pulled her up and helped her lay across the bed, hands tugging at her jeans, slowly removing the fabric from her body, revealing her beauty to me.

Naked, my mouth moved up Farrah's legs, kissing, tonguing, fingers grazing and purposefully teasing inches of her golden skin. She pushed against my mouth, seeking release as my tongue teased her center, sucking at her clit and pressing her until she became nothing more than a squirming, begging mess under me.

"Is that enough?" I asked teasingly, withdrawing a fraction to smile up at her. Her fingers wrapped in my hair, yanking my face back against her.

"Keep going!"

I chuckled, enjoying the strangled tone in her voice, the vibration of desperation that had threaded through her. I pressed my tongue against the tip of her clit, playing with light touches and hard presses, enjoying learning what made Farrah moan.

"Mm, like that," she murmured, her thighs clenching around my ears.

I flicked my tongue, rewarded when Farrah groaned, pressing her mound against my mouth, silently demanding more.

I added fingers, pressing up and curling them into her tight snatch, a ragged breath escaping her. Her slick wetness coated my fingers, her needy moans ruining me. An answering groan rumbled through my chest, my lips sucking against her clit, sending Farrah spiralling.

"Wolf!" She clawed at me, desperate and undone. "Now! Please!"

I pushed her back, wrapping her arms over my shoulders and positioning her how I wanted. How I needed.

I teased her clit with my cock, my voice unrecognisable. "Tell me you want it."

"I want your cock."

"How much?"

"A lot."

"A lot, hmm? But do you *need* it, babe?"

"Yes." The gasping admission left me harder than a diamond, my cock aching to fill her. She hungrily rubbed her clit against my cock, begging and squirming, mindless in her need. "Please, Wolf –"

I thrust hard, both of us gasping, groaning, clutching at each other as I fucked her raw.

My mouth found her shoulder, nipping and leaving a mark before soothing the bite with a kiss.

An involuntary whimper escaped her, so fucking delicious I needed to hear it again. My hips shifted, and I began to ride her, fucking into her, relishing the tight grip and pull of her spasming pussy.

"Milk my cock, babe. Squeeze me." I ordered, knowing the extra friction would push her over.

She did, clenching at my cock, a strangled scream ripping from her throat as she came.

We slumped back to the bed, a pile of sweaty, satisfied limbs.

I pressed tiny kisses to her shoulder, her neck, her cheek, the need to touch her still out of control even as my desire cooled in the aftermath of our lovemaking.

"Wolf?"

"Mm?"

She blinked one eye open, giving me a saucy grin. "That's one."

"One?" I asked, confused.

"I said we needed to make love a million times. That's officially round one."

I laughed, my body cooling even as my soul warmed.

*I'm going to marry this girl.*

"Guess I better get warmed up for round two, hey?"

"Mm, yes please."

# 15

**Farrah**

I swallowed, valiantly attempting to draw some form of moisture into my mouth.

"You ready?" Wolf asked from beside me, his guitar at the ready.

Around the globe people were beginning to log in for the live fundraiser, the chat box going crazy with fans excited for the event. I'd be opening the show in less than a minute and my nerves were off the chart.

"Not at all," I whispered, wishing the world would swallow me.

Wolf pulled me into him, wrapping his arms around my body and kissing me. "I love you. You'll be great. I promise."

Fortified by his belief in me, I turned back to

the camera that had been positioned in his recording studio.

"Ready?" Laura Sweep called from the sound desk on the other side of the glass.

I shot her a week thumbs up, too nervous to answer.

"Alright in three, two..." she pointed at me, giving me a nod.

"Hello world! And welcome to our fundraiser for the Capricorn Cove Wildlife Education and Rehabilitation Centre. I'm your host, Farrah Sharif. I also happen to be the Managing director of our centre. I'm proud to bring you this stellar line up of amazing artists from around the globe. Throughout today's program you'll be able to donate to our Centre by clicking on the buttons at the left of your screen. Every donation is tax deductible and all information is available on the links provided. We're now going to play a short clip that introduces you to our Centre."

Laura shot me a thumbs up, and I could hear the clip playing over my earphones. We'd filmed these clips over the last few days, rapidly piecing them together for this moment. They profiled some of the staff and animals at the centre and discussed the important work we did in rehabilitating the injured wildlife.

Laura held up a hand, her fingers ticking down to zero.

"And now, let me introduce my first guest. He's the lead singer of Metal Heart, currently the Centre's biggest donor, and the most wonderful human being I know. Please welcome, Wolf Rodriguez!"

The camera light switched off, letting me know that my time had finished. I swivelled on my chair, watching Wolf charm the camera.

"Thanks Farrah. And for those playing at home, yes, Farrah and I are in my recording studio and that's because she's my live-in girlfriend." He sent me a wink over the camera. "Love you, babe."

I rolled my eyes, a warm fire heating my belly.

"Don't worry, Metal Heart will be playing later, but I thought I'd kick this party off with a sneak peek at a new song. I call this one, Breath."

He looked at me over the camera, strumming his guitar as he began to sing.

*"You take my breath away*
*Every time you walk into the room*
*My heart races, I can't think*
*I'm lost in your sweet perfume*

.  .  .

BREATHE, *oh breathe*
    *I can't seem to catch my breath*
    *You're the air need to live*
    *I'm gasping for love, can't you see*
    *I want to get lost in you and me*


EVERY TOUCH, *every kiss*
    *Sends shivers down my spine*
    *I'm addicted to the way you love me*
    *I'm yours, forever and all time*


BREATHE, *oh breathe*
    *I can't seem to catch my breath*
    *You're the air that I need to live*
    *I'm drowning in love, can't you see*
    *I want to get lost in you and me*


I CAN'T IMAGINE *life without you*
    *You're the sun in my sky*
    *The air in my lung*
    *I'll love you till the end of time*


BREATHE, *oh breathe*
    *I can't seem to catch my breath*
    *You're the air that I need to live*

*I'm drowning in love, can't you see*
*I want to get lost in you and me*


*You take my breath away*
*With every word you say*
*I'm lost in your love, can't you see*
*Breath, oh breathe, you're the air I breathe.*
*I want to get lost in you and me*


*Farrah, marry me*
*Please."*

I blinked and the next thing I knew he'd discarded the guitar and was down on one knee holding out a ring box.

"Oh my gods," I whispered, staring at him with huge eyes. "What are you doing?"

"Farrah Sharif, I know this is quick but when you know, you know. You're the breath in my lungs. I love you. You give me words that no one else does. You inspire me, delight me, vex me." He held up the box. "Marry me?"

Behind the glass I could hear Laura and her crew, including Yasmin, screaming at me to say yes. Fans around the world were no doubt conflicted, some delighted, others annoyed by this PDA, and some ready to kill me for taking their man.

No one mattered except Wolf.

"Yes," I whispered, my voice breaking. "Now and forever, yes!"

Wolf rose up, wrapping me in a hug, spinning us around as he kissed my laughing mouth.

"She said yes!" he roared before kissing me again and again, his joy gratifyingly contagious.

Laura entered the recording studio, a giant grin on her face. "Congratulations!" She plucked the microphone from my hand, turning to the camera. "And on that note, let's cut to our next band. Take it away, White Oaks!"

"I love you," I whispered, kissing Wolf's gorgeous mouth once more.

"Forever and always," he agreed.

# EPILOGUE 1

**Farrah**

*Sometime in the near future...*

I stared at the cheque in my hand, blinking at the numbers. They didn't change.

*Don't lose it, Farrah. Hold it together. He's just trying to be helpful. Don't lose your cool. Don't—*

"WOLF!" I screamed, anger riding me hard. "Get your ass in here, now!"

"Oh, shit," came a muttered curse from the lounge area where Malik, Omar and Alec were all lazing around watching the game.

Wolf poked his head in from our deck, a pair of tongs in his hand. He'd been grilling ribs. "You called?"

I held up the offending letter. "You want to explain this?"

He squinted trying to read it from across the room. "Oh, is that the royalty?"

"Oh, is that the royalty?" I repeated in a snarky voice. "Yes, it's the royalty! A royalty I didn't earn!"

He rolled his eyes. "I already told you, you help me every day. Without you, none of these songs would have been written."

I could feel the steam billowing from my ears. "Wolf!"

He blew me a kiss. "Love you, babe, but this is happening. In fact, it's already happened. If it makes you this uncomfortable just give it away to charity or something. I gotta get back to the ribs."

Then my husband-to-be had the *gall* to remove himself from the conversation.

I glared at his retreating back, my ire up.

*How dare he—*

"How much is it for?" Malik asked from his seat on our sofa.

"Two hundred and fifty-nine thousand, five hundred and twenty-three dollars and nineteen cents."

He whistled. "That's a shit tone of rescued turtles."

A startled laugh broke free, the tension draining from my body. "What?"

"Turtles. You're gonna use it to rescue them, right?"

I looked down at the cheque in my hand, considering my options. Much to my surprise, Wolf's muse had continued to enjoy my ASMR attempts. To such an extent that he'd written three Grammy and two Billboard Award-winning smash hits. Unfortunately, he firmly believed I deserved to be listed as a co-writer on each and every song, entitling me to royalties I truly believed I hadn't earned.

A kick had me pressing my hand to my stomach, the little bump a reminder that I had another being to think of.

*College fund. If Wolf is going to be like this then at least I can fund this one thing.*

I grinned, knowing how much it'd piss Wolf off when he learned what I'd done.

*Serves you right, buddy.*

We'd been scheduled to get married in March of next year, but finding out we were pregnant had thrown a spanner in that plan. Instead, we'd pushed the wedding, agreeing to hold it later in the year.

I knew Wolf hated the fact I wasn't officially his wife, but every day he loved me deeper, and

I knew I didn't need a ring on my finger to prove I was his.

He returned inside with the ribs, handing them off to the hungry horde before coming to wrap his arms around me.

"You still angry?" he asked, his voice low.

"No." I squeezed him tight. "You know I just hate that you give me credit for no reason."

"And yet without you, no song would be written." He pressed a kiss to my forehead, his palm settling over my stomach. "And don't even think about using that money for a college fund. I already set one up."

I laughed, leaning into him, my heart loving him a little more.

"Love you."

"Love you too, babe. Now let's eat."

# EPILOGUE 2

**Wolf**

I watched as the mother of my child, the holder of my heart, the woman of my dreams, floated towards me dressed in a green and gold wedding saree.

A million elephants could have stampeded through this moment, and I wouldn't have noticed such was my devotion to this woman.

*You did good, Rodriguez, you lucky son of a bitch.*

She made it to me, slipping her hand into mine.

"Dearly beloved, we are gathered here today...."

The celebrant ran through the official

words, but I only listened with half an ear, my focus on my bride.

"I love you," I mouthed.

"Sex later," she mouthed back with a saucy wink, startling a laugh-free.

"And now the vows. Do you Farrah Sharif—"

"I do!"

"And so do I," I said, joining the laughter from the crowd. "Is this where we kiss?"

The celebrant rolled his eyes. "Get it over with then we can get back to the legal stuff."

I pulled my bride in, hovering for a moment above her mouth. "I love you, never more than in this moment and never less than in this moment. I'm going to love you more every day, Farrah. Thanks for choosing me."

She smiled, her eyes shiny with tears. "You're the breath in my lungs, Wolf. Without you, I cease to exist. Thanks for choosing me."

Under the afternoon sun, with only our nearest and dearest as observers, our baby boy sleeping soundly in my mother's arms, I kissed my wife, knowing this was just another milestone in our forever story.

*Finally, my wife. I like the sound of that.*

~

*Thank you so much for reading! You can grab a bonus slide of life via my website.*
*You can also continue the entire series by checking them out at*
*www.EvieMitchell.com*

*If you enter the code **EBOOK10** you can get 10% off your purchase from my website.*

*Be sure to also sign up for my newsletter or check out my website for more book news.*

# ABOUT THE AUTHOR

Evie Mitchell is a thirty-something romance author (she/her/hers) living with disability. She believes in inclusion, accessibility, and fierce romance. Her loves include steamy romance novels, her husband, their THREE sausage dogs (heaven help her), and her ever-growing collection of book-related mugs.

As a woman with a diverse work history including in areas such as emergency response, event management, human rights, disability access, and security - her books are filled with true stories (bridezillas), worst-case scenarios (malfunctioning dresses), and her favorite tropes (one-bed).

Evie specialises in fiercely inclusive happily ever afters.

# ALSO BY EVIE MITCHELL

**Capricorn Cove Series**
<u>The Shake-Up</u>
<u>Double the D</u>
<u>Muffin Top</u>
<u>The Mrs. Clause</u>
<u>New Year Knew You</u>
<u>Double Breasted</u>
<u>As You Wish</u>
<u>You Sleigh Me</u>
<u>Resolution Revolution</u>
<u>Meat Load</u>

**Larsson Siblings Series**
<u>Thunder Thighs</u>
<u>Clean Sweep</u>
<u>The X-list</u>
<u>Reality Check</u>
<u>The Christmas Contract</u>

**Dogg Pack Books**
<u>Puppy Love</u>

Bad English

The Frock Up

Pier Pressure


**All Access Series**

Knot My Type

Love Flushed


**Nameless Souls MC Series**

Runner

Wrath

Ghost

Shield


**Elliot Security Series**

Rough Edge

Bleeding Edge